The Rhythm of Riddles

Three Byomkesh Bakshi Mysteries

SARADINDU BANDYOPADHYAY

Translated from the Bengali by Arunava Sinha

Introduction by Dibakar Banerjee

PUFFIN BOOKS

PUFFIN BOOKS
Published by the Penguin Group
Penguin Books India Pvt. Ltd, 7th Floor, Infinity Tower C, DLF Cyber City, Gurgaon 122 002, Haryana, India (A Penguin Random House Company)
Penguin Group (USA) Inc., 375 Hudson Street, New York, New York 10014, USA
Penguin Group (Canada), 90 Eglinton Avenue East, Suite 700, Toronto, Ontario, M4P 2Y3, Canada
Penguin Books Ltd, 80 Strand, London WC2R 0RL, England
Penguin Ireland, 25 St Stephen's Green, Dublin 2, Ireland (a division of Penguin Books Ltd)
Penguin Group (Australia), 707 Collins Street, Melbourne, Victoria 3008, Australia Penguin Group (NZ), 67 Apollo Drive, Rosedale, Auckland 0632, New Zealand
Penguin Books (South Africa) (Pty) Ltd, Block D, Rosebank Office Park, 181 Jan Smuts Avenue, Parktown North, Johannesburg 2193, South Africa

Penguin Books Ltd, Registered Offices: 80 Strand, London WC2R 0RL, England

First published in Puffin by Penguin Books India 2012

10 9 8 7 6 5 4 3 2

ISBN 9780143331827

Typeset in Minion by Eleven Arts, New Delhi
Printed at Repro India Ltd, Navi Mumbai

A PENGUIN RANDOM HOUSE COMPANY

Contents

Introduction

Have you ever had a relative in a small town? A town smaller than the one you live in, with lesser things to do and fewer places to go to than you would expect on a holiday? A town that, having quickly exhausted its meagre gifts of entertainment and diversions, lays open its quiet ennui for you to sample?

At that point, do you manage to find a quiet window in a quiet corner in your relative's house? And before that, while exploring when no one was looking, did you stumble upon a trunk under a bed stacked with dusty, cockroach-infested books an uncle left behind, having gone away?

And in that trunk do you find books with strange, faded covers with gore—dripping letters, beautiful women screaming and dark, evil looking men grinning cruelly?

Or maybe the book is so old it doesn't have a cover picture at all. Instead, it is one of those old, tattered fabric-covered hardbacks with titles like *A_ventur_s of Dete_tive_ B___o_______ B_____i* embossed in faded gold letters that now look like dried blood smeared over a secret message . . .

You open the crackling page peppered with small bullet holes the bugs made. And there it is—written in purple fountain-pen ink now faded to pink—*To Booboon. On his thirteenth birthday. Ma. 1963.*

1963! 1963?

The window has a ledge, right? Your aunt's cook made you a nice parantha, right? And a glass of *chhaas* maybe? And the folks have gone away to visit a cousin's cousin, isn't it? The alley outside the window is deathly quiet, shining in the hard, blinding summer-break sun. The whole neighbourhood cowers into an uneasy siesta. A lone red kite flies furtively in the sky. Even the birds chirp mutedly—as if a predator is at hand, creeping upon us. You turn to the first story. *Byomkesh Arrives*. It's about a spate of murders in the neighbourhood.

Congratulations. You've just discovered the perfect way to get introduced to Byomkesh Bakshi. I should know—because that's how I did it. And I imagine many before me did the same, because the first Byomkesh stories came out in the 1930s.

This gives us two whys.

1. Why do people still read Byomkesh?

2. Why do we need a hot afternoon in a quiet house in a small town to discover Byomkesh?

Let's see.

A detective story is all about the detective, the hero—and his *atmosphere*. One cannot exist without the other.

Raymond Chandler once described a detective roughly as a good man in a bad, bad world, hiding his goodness. An idealist up to his ears in selfishness, corruption and crime; but essentially uncorrupted and incorruptible himself.

He is cynical and hard-bitten, who knows how bad this world can be. He pities innocence and yet is ready to risk his life *trying to save it.* (And the world, by the way.)

Of course, he pretends he needs the money.

Or sometimes, like Byomkesh (who never had too much of money or the use for it) he pretends he needs the mental exercise because he's too smart and bored and needs to solve a problem of life and death.

But the truth is, under all that hard-bitten cynicism and that worldly smirk there lies a hero you may count on story after story, year after year, and in my case decade after decade to do the *right thing.*

Byomkesh always, always catches the criminal. He always protects the innocent. He is never greedy for money or a BMW. He is smart. Good smart. Not bad smart—(the kind of smartness some people use to jump a queue or get an extra pizza free.) But the tough, no-nonsense smartness of figuring out things for oneself and not taking any nonsense from anyone. He is honest. He stands for truth. He even hates being called a detective. He likes 'Truth Seeker' better.

We also like to read Byomkesh because he shows us that being honest and *good smart* is way cooler than being a jumped-up idiot with a fancy car and a fancy house talking loudly in a fancy restaurant about his fancy holiday in Pattaya. (That's a place in Thailand where people sometimes go to show off, and needless to say a place Byomkesh never visited *but look! We are still reading about him!*)

And in a world where criminals sit inside parliaments, or hog prime time on television with fawning fans, or cheat other people and live on the 40th floor in eleven bedrooms—doing the *right thing* the Byomkesh way is kind of rare, isn't it?

Ace detective writers, like the creator of Byomkesh, know this secret. They know deep down we need a Byomkesh to set this wrong world right again and again.

That still leaves the window ledge unexplained. Why do we need a hot, silent afternoon dripping with menace to enjoy Byomkesh?

Remember *atmosphere?* That's the world the fictional detective operates in. The bad, evil, dangerous world he fights through. Why do we need that so badly in a good detective story?

Because you cannot tell a story about the good without describing the bad. And because you cannot make the hero win big without making his battle big.

So they do atmosphere. Bad, dangerous atmosphere. A shadowy, dark, menacing world of intrigue and devilish conspiracy. The tougher the puzzle, the harder we root for our hero when he solves the crime.

Often, that atmosphere becomes dark and shadowy quite literally. Remember all those stories and movies with dark back alleys in the night, a lone lamppost blinking in the fog and a black car with hooded headlights? Mere setting for our detective hero. Makes him look good.

But there is a subtler, smarter variety of the dangerous world that smarter detectives and their creators, like Byomkesh and Saradindu Banerjee, inhabit as atmosphere. The everyday world right outside your window. The street in front of your house. Your friend's uncle's bungalow in Ooty, or Darjeeling, or Ranchi. A book shop. A sanatorium. A lone cyclist cycling down an empty street. A letter. A boarding house. Evil and criminal masterminds lurk right out there in the world you thought was so familiar. And when Byomkesh unmasks some devilish criminal right in the midst of his benign neighbours, you shudder harder. Who knew? Who could have thought?

It's real. Like your relative's window ledge. Like the hot, lazy afternoon. That intermittent bird calling could be the arch criminal calling his henchmen to move in. Or that red kite up in the sky could be the signal that murder has been committed. Anything is possible. And all this while tea is being served!

Byomkesh's world is very ordinary. Very middle class. What's more, very, very Indian. He doesn't wear a fedora hat or a tacky overcoat on rent from Maganlal Dresswala (like most filmy detectives who copy the American gumshoe). He wears the ordinary dhoti kurta of the Bengali bhadralok. He may walk out to the street corner shop for an after dinner *meetha paan* while solving a grisly murder. What's more, his nemesis, the arch criminal, might be quite content to have a nice meal of fish curry and rice before planning world domination or the cocaine monopoly of the eastern hemisphere with chilling, cold-blooded efficiency.

Real people are villains here. People you and I could know easily in our ordinary lives. Yet these very ordinary, real people, unknown to us, are planning something horribly twisted.

And in story after story, like the ones in this book, Byomkesh's mind runs faster than light and cuts sharper than a Teflon razor to bring these diabolical criminal to justice. No shoot-outs. No car chases. No explosions. Just a brain. Lot of logic and courage. And the will to expose the truth. And that makes Byomkesh not only look good, and *good smart*—but *real.*

As real as that window ledge in a sleepy little town. Because at the time they were written, they were commonplace. Booboon, sitting on that ledge in 1963, would have felt the real, immediate thrill of Byomkesh's adventures.

I'm convinced that if Saradindu had written Byomkesh today, he would have been taking the metro or checking out the nearest multiplex for clues to catch the murderer. The villain would have worn cargo shorts. And you would have felt the thrill in your bones just as if it was happening to you.

And if you've bought this book off the Net or at the nearest mall and don't have that window ledge in your flat, do not despair. All you need to do is to imagine that there is real nasty business happening out there and there's someone real smart to stop it. That's what Booboon felt in 1963 as he curled up with *his* Byomkesh.

The truth is, a real, convincing detective doing extraordinary things in an ordinary world works in every age.

Because without people like Byomkesh, it'll be a bad, bad world to live in. It was true in 1963. And it's true now.

Hopefully, it will be for a long time to come.

May 2012 Dibakar Banerjee

The Rhythm of Riddles

1

Byomkesh had been to Cuttack on official work, I had accompanied him too. After a few days, it became evident that the task would not be accomplished quickly, that it would take time to rummage through a mountain of deeds and documents in the government office to unearth the truth. Accordingly, Byomkesh stayed on in Cuttack, while I returned to Calcutta. How could a Bengali household be expected to run without the presence of a man at home?

On my return to Calcutta, however, I had no work. I was feeling a little helpless in Byomkesh's absence. Winter was setting in, the days were getting shorter; and yet the hours refused to pass. Occasionally I would visit the shop, supervise Prabhat, who ran the shop, read new manuscripts if any. But still there was nothing to do for most part of the day.

Then an opportunity to pass the evenings presented itself unexpectedly.

We lived in a three-storied building, occupying five rooms on the top floor, while a dozen or so office goers messed together on the first floor. On the ground floor were the manager's room, the pantry, the kitchen and the dining room, with just one corner room being occupied by a solitary boarder. We were familiar with all of them, but not particularly intimate with any.

That evening, I had just switched on the light after darkness had fallen and opened a magazine when there was a knock on the door. Opening the door, I discovered a middle-aged gentleman standing outside, smiling deferentially. I had seen him once or twice on the first floor of our building, where he had taken up residence recently. He occupied the best corner room on the floor all by himself. He appeared to be a man of refined tastes, being dressed in a warm Nehru jacket and a silk churidar, his hair more black than white. He was well turned out.

Greeting me, he said, 'Excuse me, my name is Bhupesh Chatterjee. I live on the first floor.'

'I've seen you now and then,' I replied, 'though I was not familiar with your name. Do come in.'

I gave him a seat in my room. 'I came to Calcutta a month-and-a-half ago. I work for an insurance company; there's no telling where I'll be next. Tomorrow they might transfer me somewhere else altogether, for all you know.'

'You work for an insurance company,' I said with some

unease. 'But I have never taken out a policy, nor am I planning to.'

'That's not what I came for,' he smiled. 'It's true that I work at the insurance office, but I'm not an agent. I came because . . .' After an awkward pause, he said, 'I'm addicted to bridge. I haven't had a game ever since I came here, I'm dying for one. After much effort I've managed to find two more players. They live in Room No. 3 on the first floor. But we haven't been able to find a fourth. We tried cutthroat bridge for a few days, but it isn't the real thing. I thought I'd find out today whether Ajit-babu is interested.'

I was indeed interested in bridge once upon a time. Not merely interested, obsessed. Since I had not played for a long time, the obsession had died. Still, I felt that playing bridge was preferable to passing my companionless evenings reading a dull magazine.

'Very well, very well,' I said. 'I am long out of practice, of course, but still—why not?'

'Then come with me,' said Bhupesh-babu, springing to his feet. 'I have made all the arrangements in my room. Why waste time?'

'Please lead the way, I'll follow as soon as I've had my cup of tea,' I said.

'Oh no, you can just as well have your tea in my room. Come along,' he replied.

I was amused by his eagerness. I used to be just as enthusiastic once upon a time; the evenings seemed wasted without a game of bridge.

I got off my chair. Informing Byomkesh's wife Satyabati, I accompanied Bhupesh-babu downstairs.

The first room when you went down the stairs to the first floor was Bhupesh-babu's. Pausing near his door, he called out loudly, 'Come along, Ram-babu, Banamali-babu. I've got hold of Ajit-babu.'

Two heads popped out of Room No. 3, which was situated halfway down the corridor, then disappeared with the word, 'Coming.' Bhupesh-babu took me into his room and switched on the light.

It was a commodious room. There were two barred windows on the wall looking out on the road. On one side of the room was the bed, covered with a bedspread, on the other was a cupboard, on top of which reposed a shining portable stove and everything you needed to make a cup of tea. Four chairs were arranged around a low table in the middle of the room; it was clearly a card table. Besides these, the other small items of furniture, including a dressing table and a chest of drawers, all indicated good taste. Bhupesh-babu was slightly Western in his tastes.

Settling me in a chair, he said, 'Let me put the kettle on, the tea will be ready in a few minutes.'

Lighting the stove, he put the kettle on. Meanwhile, Ram-babu and Banamali-babu had arrived.

Despite our prior acquaintance, Bhupesh-babu introduced all of us once more. 'This is Ramchandra Roy, and this is Banamali Chanda. They live in the same room and work at the same bank.'

I observed other similarities too; I had not noticed them earlier, possibly because I had not seen them together. Both were aged between forty-five and fifty, both were plump and of medium height, their features cut in the same mould—a thick nose, invisible eyebrows, a square chin. The resemblance was obviously genetic. I was tempted to surprise them. After all, I was a friend of Byomkesh's.

'Are you related?' I asked.

They looked at me in surprise. 'No,' answered Ram-babu a little brusquely. 'I'm a vaidya, Banamali is a kayastha.'

I was taken aback. Just as I was trying to stammer out an explanation, Bhupesh-babu arrived with a plate of snacks to rescue me. Then the tea arrived. Finishing our tea quickly, we got down to the game. The subject of their being cousins was forgotten.

As we played I discovered I had not forgotten the art of bridge even after all these years; my playing and bidding expertise were both intact. The stakes were low; the most one could win or lose at the end of the rubber was four annas. But playing was no fun without stakes.

Ram-babu and I were partners in the first round—or rubber. Ram-babu lit a thick cigar, Bhupesh-babu and I lit our cigarettes; Banamali-babu was content with slices of clove and betelnut.

Then we began to play. After every rubber, the cards were shuffled and the pairs, changed. All three of them were good players; there wasn't much conversation as everyone was immersed in the game. Only the ends of the cigar and the cigarettes glowed constantly. Bhupesh-babu rose at one point to open the window and resumed his seat in silence.

When we finished our game, it was past nine; the servant had already reminded everyone twice of dinner. When we totted up, I turned out to have won two annas. Pocketing my winnings, I rose to my feet joyfully. 'We'll play again tomorrow, won't we?' asked Bhupesh-babu with a smile.

'We will,' I said.

When I went back upstairs, Satyabati remonstrated with me. Nine-fifteen on a winter night was quite late. But, happy after a game of bridge after such a long time, I laughed away her scolding.

After this our games became a daily affair, the session beginning as soon as the evening lamp was lit and continuing until nine at night. After five or six days, I had formed an impression about each of them. Bhupesh-babu was kind-hearted, soft-spoken and hospitable, extremely fond of bridge. Ram-babu was grave, taciturn, not given to protesting against others' mistakes while playing. Banamali-babu held Ram-babu in the greatest of regard, trying without success to emulate his gravity. Both were reticent, deeply addicted to bridge. Both had faint Eastern Bengali accents.

We had been happily playing bridge for six days, our sessions on the verge of becoming a permanent institution, when a ghastly incident on the floor below upset our regular gathering. Natabar Nashkar, the only inhabitant of the ground floor, was suddenly murdered. While it is true that we had no direct relationship with him, even when a ship sails along the middle of the river the waves do reach the banks.

At six-thirty that evening, I was on my way to our evening game, wrapped in a shawl. Because I was a little late, I ran down the stairs, my sandals flapping loudly. Just as I had reached the last step, a bang made me stop in my tracks. I could not identify the source of the sound. It could have been a car backfiring out on the street, but the sound was rather loud. No sound from the street could be as deafening.

After a brief halt I continued on to Bhupesh-babu's room. The lights were on. Bhupesh-babu was looking out through the window, holding the bars, while behind him Ram-babu and Banamali-babu were trying to peep through the same window. When I entered, Bhupesh-babu was saying excitedly, 'There . . . there . . . he ran out of the lane just this minute, did you see him? He had a brown shawl on . . .'

'What's the matter?' I said from the back.

Everyone turned towards me. 'Did you hear the sound?' asked Bhupesh-babu. 'It came from the lane beneath this window here. I'd just opened the window when there was a bang down there. I looked out and saw a man running out of the lane.'

Our building was situated on the main road. A narrow, paved blind lane connected the road to our back door;

the servants took this route in and out of the house. I felt a misgiving. 'The room beneath this one is occupied. The sound didn't come from that room, did it?'

'No idea,' said Bhupesh-babu. 'Someone does live in the room beneath mine, but I don't know his name.'

Ram-babu and Banamali-babu exchanged glances, after which Ram-babu cleared his throat and said, 'The room downstairs is occupied by Natabar Nashkar.'

'Let's go and see,' I said. 'If he's in he can tell us what the sound was.'

None of the three seemed keen, but I was Byomkesh the truth-seeker's friend. How could I not investigate the source of the sound? 'Let's take a quick look before we start our game,' I said. 'I wouldn't have bothered if it had been an everyday sort of sound, but even if someone came through the lane to throw a cracker into Natabar-babu's room we should find out, shouldn't we?'

They accompanied me reluctantly.

There was a lock on the manager Shibkali-babu's door, and the door to the pantry was shut too. The dining room was unlocked, for it held nothing but a few low stools. Only the door to Natabar-babu's room was closed without being locked. It would not be incorrect to presume that he was in, therefore. 'Natabar-babu!' I called out.

There was no reply. When a relatively louder call did not elicit a response either, I pushed on the door gently. The doors parted slightly.

The room was dark, nothing was visible; but there was

a faint smell. The smell of gunpowder. We exchanged startled looks.

'There must be a switch by the door,' sad Bhupesh-babu. 'Wait, let me turn on the light.'

Pushing me aside he peeped into the room, then reached in to grope for the switch. There was a click, and the light came on.

The first thing we saw in the unforgiving overhead light was Natabar-babu's corpse. Dressed in a white sweater and a dhoti, he lay on his back in the middle of the room, his limbs splayed out. A thick stream of blood had flowed out of the area near his chest. Natabar Nashkar had not been particularly handsome even when alive; he was of medium build with a protruding stomach, his bloated face deeply pockmarked. But death had made his appearance even more grotesque. I shall not describe that horror. You could tell from his expression how hideous an emotion the fear of death is.

Frozen briefly into a statue by the sight, Ram-babu emitted a sound like a hiccup from his throat. He stared at the corpse with unbelieving eyes, as if in a trance. Suddenly sinking his nails into Ram-babu's arms, Banamali-babu said, 'He's dead, dada!' It wasn't clear to me whether his expression was one of sorrow or wonder or joy.

'There's no doubt he's dead,' Bhupesh-babu said, his face pale. 'He died of a gunshot. There. Can you see it on the window sill?'

The window, which had no bars, was open—on its sill lay a pistol. The picture became clear; standing outside the window, the assailant had shot Natabar Nashkar, then left after depositing the pistol on the window sill.

Hearing quick footsteps behind me, I turned. Shibkali Chakraborty, the manager of the boarding house, was approaching. He had an emaciated frame, he walked with undue haste, his eyes were unnecessarily distraught; when he spoke, he wasn't satisfied unless he had repeated himself several times. 'All of you here? Here? What's the matter? What's the matter?' he said when he was near us.

'See for yourself.' We moved away from the door to give him a clear view. Shibkali-babu jumped out of his skin when he saw the blood-soaked corpse. 'Oh my god, oh my god. Natabar Nashkar is dead. Blood, blood. How did he die?'

'You can find out for yourself over there,' I said, pointing at the window.

'Oh god, a pistol, a pistol,' Shibkali-babu babbled again in terror as soon as he saw the gun. 'Natabar-babu has been murdered with a pistol. Who murdered him? When was he murdered?'

'I have no idea who murdered him,' I replied, 'but I do know when he was murdered. About five minutes ago.'

I explained everything to him briefly. He stared at the corpse in distress.

I had not noticed earlier, but suddenly I realized that Shibkali-babu was dressed in a brown shawl. My heart leapt into my mouth. Controlling my palpitations, I said, 'Weren't you home? Did you go out?'

'What? Yes I . . . was out on work,' he replied in agitation. 'But . . . but . . . what is the way out? What is to be done . . . what is to be done?'

'The first thing to be done is to inform the police,' I said.

'True, true,' responded Shibkali-babu. 'That's right, that's right. But I do not have a telephone. You have a telephone, Ajit-babu, if you could . . .'

'I shall telephone the police immediately,' I said. 'But none of you must enter the room; wait here till the police arrive.'

I dashed upstairs. As I was about to enter my room I saw my own reflection in the mirror. I was dressed in a brown shawl too.

We were acquainted with Pranab Guha, the police-inspector in our locality at that time. A competent, middle-aged man, he was not, however, favourably inclined towards Byomkesh. While he did not express his amiability in any manner of harshness of speech or rudeness, he spoke to Byomkesh with excessive obsequiousness, chuckling softly at the end. Possibly their natures were mutually abhorrent; besides, Pranab-babu did not care for the coarse touch of an unofficial hand in official matters.

Having listened to my account on the telephone, he said sarcastically, 'Really! A crime in the detective's den! But when you have Byomkesh-babu there, why do you need me? Let him conduct the investigation.'

'Byomkesh is not in Calcutta,' I said testily. 'Had he been here, he would definitely have taken up the case.'

'Oh all right, I'll come round then,' said Inspector Pranab. He put the phone down with a chuckle. I went back downstairs.

Pranab-babu arrived with his entourage half-an-hour later. He chuckled when he caught sight of me, then inspected the corpse gravely. Lifting the pistol gingerly from the window sill, he wrapped it in his handkerchief and put it in his pocket. Eventually, having dispatched the corpse, he occupied the only chair in the room and proceeded to interrogate all the inmates of the house.

I told him whatever I knew. I am summarizing the statements of the others—

Shibkali-babu, the manager, was sworn to a vow of celibacy—a bachelor, in other words. He had been running the boarding house for the past twenty-five years; it was his wife, his child, his family . . . Natabar Nashkar had taken up residence in this ground floor room three years earlier, and had occupied it ever since. He was approximately fifty years of age, and not given to consorting with the others. Ram-babu and Banamali-babu used to visit him in his room once in a while. Shibkali-babu bore no ill-will towards Natabar Nashkar, for Natabar paid his dues promptly on the first of every month . . . Shibkali-babu had learnt that afternoon of potatoes being sold cheap at a particular warehouse, so he had gone to the godown to purchase potatoes. But the potatoes had been sold out already, so he had returned empty-handed.

Bhupesh-babu worked at an insurance office; he had

been transferred to Calcutta a month-and-a-half earlier. He was about forty-five, a widower with no children. He had no home to speak of; he had travelled all over the country in course of work. Bhupesh-babu gave an accurate account of how he had gathered a group of people to play bridge, and of that evening's incidents; he mentioned the man in the brown shawl too. He had not seen the man's face clearly; from the back you cannot see the face of a man who is running away; so he was unlikely to recognize the man were he to see him again.

The statements given by Ramchandra Roy and Banamali Chanda were similar. I observed that although Ram-babu remained composed throughout the questioning, Banamali-babu appeared somewhat perturbed. Both of them used to live in Dhaka earlier, working in the same British firm. Their wives, children and family had all been killed in the riots at the time of the Partition, and they had somehow managed to escape with their lives. Ram-babu was forty-eight years old; Banamali-babu, forty-five. They had lived in this boarding house after crossing over to Calcutta, and worked in a bank. Three years had passed this way.

They were fond of playing bridge, but had not had an opportunity to play since moving to Calcutta. Bhupesh-babu had made arrangements for bridge in his room a few days earlier, and the evenings had been passing pleasantly since then. Within five minutes of their entering Bhupesh-babu's room this evening, there was the sound of an explosion in the lane outside . . . They had been acquainted with Natabar-babu in Dhaka; it had been a slight acquaintance, without any particular closeness. Natabar-babu had worked as an agent for various enterprises in Dhaka. By virtue of living in the same boarding house, they used to meet occasionally; Ram-babu and Banamali-babu would drop in for a chat. They did not know whether Natabar-babu had any other friends . . . They had seen the man in the brown shawl for a split second in the dim light of dusk at the head of the lane; they would not be able to recognize him again.

The remaining inmates were unable to reveal anything. A game of dice had been in progress in a room at the other end of the first floor. Four players and four other spectators had been present there; they had not heard the gunshot. No one else in the boarding house had anything more than a nodding acquaintance with Natabar-babu.

Only the servant Haripada said something that could be either irrelevant or significant. At six in the evening, Suren-babu from the first floor had sent Haripada to the restaurant on the main road to buy some snacks. On his way back through the back lane, Haripada had heard someone murmuring in Natabar-babu's room. He had been unable to see who was inside because the door had been shut; nor had he recognized the voice. Haripada had noticed this specifically because Natabar-babu did not usually have many visitors. He could not specify the time, but Suren-babu stated clearly that he had asked Haripada to get the snacks at six in the evening.

In other words, Natabar-babu had had a visitor in his room half an hour before he died. It wasn't anyone in the boarding house, for no one admitted visiting him. Therefore it had been an outsider. Perhaps it had been the man in the brown shawl. Or some other person altogether; Haripada's statement proved nothing.

After he had taken everyone's testimony, Inspector Pranab said, 'All of you may leave now, we will search the room. And yes, this is for Ajit-babu and Shibkali-babu—do not attempt to leave Calcutta without my permission until this murder mystery is solved.'

'What do you mean?' I asked in surprise.

'I mean that both you and Shibkali-babu are dressed in brown shawls,' answered Inspector Pranab. 'Heh heh. You may leave now.'

He slammed the door on our faces. We returned to our respective burrows. The game of cards was forgotten.

The following day passed in inactive tedium. The police made no noise. Inspector Pranab had left the previous evening with some documents after searching Natabar-babu's room and locking the door. The man was hostile towards us, but he expressed his hostility so courteously that you could say nothing. He knew I had a watertight alibi, but had still used a flimsy pretext to issue instructions forbidding me to leave Calcutta. Since I was a friend of Byomkesh's, harassing me was his only motive.

In the morning, the gentlemen at the boarding house all left for their respective offices. No one seemed the slightest bit perturbed. There was no regret amongst any of them for the death by gunshot of a person named Natabar Nashkar, who had lived in the same boarding house for three years. 'If thou beest born, die thou must'—everyone appeared to harbour a philosophical attitude.

In the evening I went to Bhupesh-babu's room. Rambabu and Banamali-babu had turned up as well. All of us seemed to be lacking in spirit. No one suggested a rubber. Our session broke up after miserably discussing Natabar Nashkar's death and criticizing the incompetence of the police over a cup of tea.

As I climbed the stairs, a thought occurred to me. No matter how efficient Inspector Pranab was, he would not be able to solve the mystery of Natabar-babu's death. Byomkesh wasn't here; the evening sessions were flagging. It would not be a bad idea to write an account of the entire affair instead of sitting by idly. I would have something to do, and maybe Byomkesh would be able to get to the bottom of the matter if he could read my account when he returned.

I began writing that very night. Starting at the beginning, I wrote down every last detail from my perspective in a way that would not allow Byomkesh to pick holes in the narrative. I finished writing the next afternoon.

I may have finished writing, but the story was not finished. Who knew when and where the story of Natabar-babu's murder would end? Maybe the murderer's identity would never be known. Feeling somewhat dissatisfied, I had barely lit a cigarette when Byomkesh strolled in holding his suitcase.

'Byomkesh! You're back!' I jumped to my feet. 'So your work's done?'

'The work's not even begun,' Byomkesh said. 'Two government departments are at loggerheads with each other. Each wants to be the first to lay down its life for the cause. When I saw all this I decided to leave. I'll go back when they've finished battling each other.'

Hearing Byomkesh's voice, Satyabati came running, wiping her hand on the end of her sari. They were not newlyweds any more, but even now a joyful light appeared in Satyabati's eyes when Byomkesh appeared unexpectedly.

When the couple's reunion was over I brought up the subject of Natabar's murder and gave Byomkesh what I had written for him to read. Byomkesh started reading my notes over a cup of tea.

He returned it to me at six in the evening, saying, 'So Inspector Pranab has confined you to the city. What the fellow must think of us! We shall meet him tomorrow. Let us go and meet Bhupesh-babu now.'

I realized the case had intrigued Byomkesh. 'By all means,' I said, pleased. 'We may run into Ram-babu and Banamali-babu too.'

I took Byomkesh to Bhupesh-babu's room on the first floor. My assumption had not been incorrect; Ram-babu and Banamali-babu were indeed there. Byomkesh did not have to be introduced to anyone, for everyone knew who he was. Bhupesh-babu welcomed him warmly, and put the kettle on for tea. Ram-babu's gravity remained intact, but a nervous wariness was occasionally evident in Banamali's eyes.

Taking a seat, Byomkesh said, 'I was once addicted to bridge. Then Ajit taught me chess. But now I no longer enjoy playing.'

Turning to look at him as he was putting the tea leaves into the boiling water in the kettle, Bhupesh-babu said, 'Now for only the sport unto death with my life.'

I was startled to hear Bhupesh-babu quote Rabindranath Tagore. He not only worked at the insurance office but also read poetry!

'Right you are,' responded Byomkesh quietly. 'Playing against death all my life has ensured that I can no longer train my mind on light-hearted games.'

'It's different for you,' answered Bhupesh-babu. 'I deal in death too; what else is insurance but the business of death. But I still enjoy bridge.'

Byomkesh may have been talking to Bhupesh-babu, but his eyes kept drifting towards Ram-babu and Banamali-babu. They sat in silence, unfamiliar with such light but refined conversation.

Bhupesh-babu brought the cups of tea and a plate of cream crackers. 'Yours is a different kind of personality too. Bridge is a game for the intelligent; those who are intelligent are naturally attracted to this game. Some people play bridge as a means of respite from the agony of living. Many years ago I knew someone who used to play bridge to forget the agony of his son's death.'

Three pairs of eyes turned mechanically towards Byomkesh. No one spoke, all of them could only stare in surprise. A heavy silence descended on the room.

We finished our cups of tea without a word. Then Byomkesh broke the silence and said matter-of-factly, 'I was in Cuttack, I have only just got back. Ajit informed me of Natabar Nashkar's death as soon as I arrived. I was not acquainted with Natabar-babu, but the news of his death made me curious. You do not often have a murder on your own doorstep. So I thought of making your acquaintance.'

'How fortunate then that the murder took place,' said Bhupesh-babu, 'or else you'd never have graced my room. But I know nothing about Natabar Nashkar. I had never even set eyes on him when he was alive. Ram-babu and Banamali-babu knew him a little.'

Byomkesh looked at Ram-babu. A shadow of fear seemed to fall over his gravity. He fidgeted, cleared his throat as though about to say something, then shut his mouth. Thereupon Byomkesh turned his glance towards Banamali-babu, saying, 'I'm sure you know what kind of a man Natabar-babu was.'

Startled, Banamali-babu stammered, 'Uh . . . ar . . . he wasn't a bad sort . . . quite a decent sort, in fact . . . but . . .'

Ram-babu finally regained his power of speech, cutting in on Banamali-babu's incomplete sentence.

'Look, we were by no means friends of Natabar-babu's. But when we lived in Dhaka, he lived next door to us, so we were acquainted. We know nothing about his character.'

'How long ago did you live in Dhaka?' asked Byomkesh.

'Five or six years ago,' answered Ram-babu, gulping. 'Then the Partition riots began, and we came away to West Bengal.'

'So you worked in the same firm in Dhaka?' Byomkesh asked Banamali-babu.

'Yes we did,' he answered. 'You must have heard of Godfrey-Brown; it's a large British firm. That was where . . .'

Before he could finish, Ram-babu suddenly rose from his chair. 'You haven't forgotten we have to call on Narayan-babu at seven, have you, Banamali? . . . We shall take your leave now.'

Ram-babu made a quick exit, with Banamali-babu in tow. Byomkesh turned to watch their act of retreat.

Bhupesh-babu smiled. 'Your questions sound innocuous, Byomkesh-babu,' he said, 'but Ram-babu's offended.'

'I cannot understand why,' answered Byomkesh innocently. 'Do you have any idea?'

'I have no idea,' Bhupesh-babu shook his head. 'I was in fact in Dhaka during the riots, but I didn't know any of them at the time. I know nothing about their past either.'

'You were in Dhaka too during the riots?'

'Yes, I'd been transferred to Dhaka about a year before the riots. I returned after the Partition.'

Silence reigned for some time. Byomkesh lit a cigarette.

Looking at him for a few minutes, Bhupesh-babu asked, 'Is your story about the man who used to play bridge to forget the pain of losing his son true, Byomkesh-babu?'

'Yes, it's a true story,' Byomkesh told him. 'It happened a long time ago, when I was in college. Why do you ask?'

Bhupesh-babu did not answer. Instead, he rose and fetched a photograph from his drawer, handing it to Byomkesh. It was a photo of a boy of nine or ten; his face glowing with the brightness of a child. 'My son,' Bhupesh-babu mumbled.

'Your son . . .' Byomkesh said, raising his eyes from the photograph to look at Bhupesh-babu in anxiety.

'He's dead,' Bhupesh-babu shook his head. 'He had gone to school the day the riots began in Dhaka; he never returned.'

Breaking the unbearable silence, Byomkesh asked half a question. 'Your wife . . .'

'She's dead too,' answered Bhupesh-babu. 'Her heart was weak, she couldn't bear her son's death. I neither died, nor succeeded in forgetting. It's been five or six years, I should have forgotten by now. I go to work, play cards, laugh and joke, but I cannot forget. Is there a medicine to wipe out memories of grief, Byomkesh-babu?'

'Eternity is the only medicine,' Byomkesh sighed.

2

'Let us call on Swami Pranabananda,' said Byomkesh over our morning tea the next day.

I was already under a pall of gloom after hearing of the tragedy of Bhupesh-babu's life the previous night; the thought of an encounter with Inspector Pranab depressed me further. 'Is a meeting with Pranabananda absolutely imperative?' I enquired.

'Not if you do not wish to be free of police suspicion,' answered Byomkesh.

'Very well then.'

Taking the stairs to the first floor at nine-thirty, we observed a lock on Bhupesh-babu's door. He must have gone to office. Ram-babu and Banamali-babu were emerging from their room in full finery—they retreated on seeing us. Throwing me a sidelong glance, Byomkesh smiled.

Shibkali-babu was going over the account books in his office downstairs. When he saw Byomkesh he leapt to the door, asking with anguish in his eyes, 'Byomkesh-babu! When did you return from Cuttack—what time? Have you heard about Natabar Nashkar! And now look, the police have involved me in the case—they've involved me.'

'Not just you, they have involved Ajit too,' said Byomkesh.

'Yes of course, of course. Brown shawl. Ridiculous . . . ridiculous. You must save us.'

'I shall try.'

Suddenly stopping on the road, Byomkesh said, 'Come, let us take a look at the lane.'

He was referring to the lane that ran past our home, the one down which the man in the brown shawl had escaped after shooting Natabar-babu. It was so narrow that two people couldn't walk abreast in it. We entered the lane in single file. Byomkesh advanced slowly, his eyes fixed on the paved surface. I didn't know what he had in mind, but it was rather far-fetched to expect clues to the murder three days afterwards.

The window to Natabar-babu's room was shut. Pausing before it, Byomkesh trained his probing eyes on the paved surface of the lane. The window was at a height of four feet from the ground; it would be easy to fire into the room if the shutters were open.

'What's that stain?'

Following the direction of Byomkesh's finger, I observed a discoloured mark on the ground; star shaped, with a diameter of about three inches. The lane was swept from time to time, but despite the urgency of all the cleaning, the stain had not been obliterated. It appeared to be two or three days old.

'What *is* that stain?' I asked.

Without answering, Byomkesh suddenly lowered himself to the ground like someone doing push-up exercises and planted his nose on the stain. 'What on earth are you doing?' I asked in surprise. 'Why are you rubbing your nose on the ground?'

'I was not rubbing my nose,' said Byomkesh, back on his feet. 'I was sniffing it.'

'Sniffing it! How does it smell?'

'You can sniff if too if you'd like to know.'

'No need.'

'Then let us go to the police station.'

Leaving the lane behind us, we went off towards the police station. I glanced at Byomkesh once or twice out of the corner of my eyes, but it wasn't clear whether he had discovered anything after sniffing the road.

Inspector Pranab was lording it over the police station. He was, on the whole, of pleasing appearance, medium build, and not too dark a complexion; the only flaw was that he was barely five feet three inches in height.

At the sight of Byomkesh walking in, his eyes first expressed surprise, followed by feigned humility. 'Byomkesh-babu!' he exclaimed. 'How fortunate I am to be in your august company first thing in the morning. Hehe.'

'I am no less fortunate,' countered Byomkesh. 'The scriptures clearly state the outcome of seeing a dwarf in the morning—you are freed from the cycle of rebirth.'

Inspector Pranab was taken aback. Byomkesh had always ignored his jibes, but today he was in a different frame of mind. Unprepared for a riposte, Pranab-babu said glumly, 'I admit my appearance does not resemble a lamppost.'

'You have no choice but to admit it,' Byomkesh smiled. 'Lampposts have lights on their heads; that is where they differ from you.'

Pranab-babu's face fell. Forcing out a laugh, he said, 'I can't help it; not everyone is so bright inside their heads, after all. Was there anything you needed?'

'Of course there is,' said Byomkesh. 'First, I have marched Ajit to the police station to prove to you that he is not absconding. You may rest assured that he is under my surveillance; he will not be able to escape under my nose.'

Pranab-babu attempted a disarming laugh. 'I do not know what the Commissioner will say if he learns that you have restrained Ajit from leaving the city,' Byomkesh continued without mercy, 'but I would certainly like to know. We have courts of law in this country; even police officers can be punished for unnecessarily interfering with individual freedom. But still, all that can come later. My second question is whether you have been able to gather any information concerning Natabar Nashkar's death.'

Pranab-babu debated whether to answer this question rudely. But realizing that it would not be wise to antagonize Byomkesh in his current frame of mind, he answered calmly, 'Do you have any idea of the population of Calcutta, Byomkesh-babu?'

'I have never counted,' answered Byomkesh contemptuously. 'Probably five million or so.'

'Let's say it is five million,' said Pranab-babu. 'Is it a simple task to apprehend an individual in a brown shawl from these teeming millions? Can you do it?'

'I might be able to if I have all the information.'

'Although it is against our rules to share information with outsiders, I can tell you all I know.'

'Very well, do so. Has Natabar Nashkar's family been located?'

'No. We had advertised in the papers, but no one has come forward.'

'What did the postmortem reveal?'

'The bullet penetrated the ribs to enter the heart. The bullet was matched with the gun; it was the same pistol.'

'Anything else?'

'He was quite healthy, but on the verge of developing cataract in his eyes.'

'Who's the owner of the pistol?'

'It's an American army pistol, available on the black market. There's no way in which to identify the owner.'

'Did you discover anything significant when you searched the room?'

'All the relevant items are there on that table. A diary, about five rupees in cash, a bank passbook, and a true copy of a court judgement. You may take a look if you like.'

There was a table in the corner of the room. Byomkesh went up to it, but I did not. Inspector Pranab was not a decent sort; an unpleasant situation would arise if he objected. From my chair, I saw Byomkesh examine the bank passbook, leaf through the diary, and read the court document with the judicial stamp carefully. 'I have seen all I had to,' he said on his return.

By then, the devil in Inspector Pranab had awoken again. Peering at Byomkesh, he said, 'You saw exactly what I did. Have you got to know the name and address of the culprit?'

'Yes, I have,' Byomkesh told him.

'Really!' exclaimed Pranab-babu, his eyebrows shooting skywards. 'So soon! You're incredibly clever! Would you be so good as to reveal the culprit's name, so that I may arrest him?'

'I shall not reveal the culprit's name to you, Pranab-babu,' Byomkesh said, tightening his jaw. 'That is my own discovery. You are paid a salary for your work; you will have to find out on your own. But I can offer you some help. Search the lane running beside the building.'

'Has the culprit left his footprint in there! Hehe.'

'No he has left a mark even more incriminating . . . One more thing. I shall be taking Ajit to Cuttack with me in a few days. Stop him if you dare . . . Come, Ajit.'

'Have you really identified the culprit?' I asked in excitement when we left the police station.

'I had identified him even before we came to the police station,' Byomkesh nodded, 'but Inspector Pranab is a good-for-nothing. He is not unintelligent, but his intelligence is destructive. He will never be able to get to the bottom of Natabar's murder mystery.'

'Who murdered Natabar Nashkar? Was it someone we know?' I asked.

'I shall tell you later. For now, let me tell you that Natabar Nashkar was a blackmailer by profession. You had better go back home, I am going to the city. Godfrey-Brown has a large office here in Calcutta too. I might get some information there. It may be some time before I am back.' He left with a wave.

I returned home alone. It was 1.30 by the time Byomkesh came back.

'You have to do something for me,' he said after his bath and lunch. 'You have to invite Ram-babu, Banamali-babu and Bhupesh-babu to tea. We shall gather here in this room this evening.'

'Very well. But what's going on? Why did you go to the Godfrey-Brown office?'

'There was a court judgement among Natabar Nashkar's belongings at the police station. When I read it I discovered that two brothers named Rashbehari Biswas and Banabehari Biswas were the treasurer and assistant-treasurer, respectively, at the Dhaka office of Godfrey-Brown. They were caught embezzling funds seven years ago. They were taken to court. Banabehari was sentenced to two years' imprisonment, and Rashbehari, to three. Natabar Nashkar had got hold of this judgement. Then his diary revealed that he used to get eighty rupees every month from Rashbehari and Banabehari Biswas. I went to Godfrey-Brown to verify the misappropriation of funds. It is true. I had no more doubts that Natabar was blackmailing them.'

'But . . . Rashebehari, Banabehari . . . who are they? Where will you find them?'

'They aren't far away; you only have to go as far as Room No. 3.'

'What! Ram-babu and Banamali-babu!'

'Yes. You came close to the truth. They are not just related, they are brothers. To honour the idiom, you could say they are not just brothers-in-arms but also thick as thieves.'

'But . . . but . . . they could not have murdered Natabar. When Natabar was killed they were . . .'

'Patience,' said Byomkesh, raising his hand. 'You shall hear the whole story at tea.'

A variety of snacks bought from the Marwari store and tea had been prepared to entertain the guests. Bhupesh-babu was the first to arrive. Dressed in a dhoti and kurta, he had a folded grey shawl over his shoulder and an eager smile on his face. 'Have you made arrangements for bridge too?' he asked.

'We can make arrangements if everyone wants to play,' Byomkesh replied.

Ram-babu and Banamali-babu arrived a little later, their coats buttoned up to their necks, their eyes wary. 'Welcome, welcome,' said Byomkesh.

Byomkesh led a witty conversation over the tea and snacks. I observed after some time that Ram-babu and Banamali-babu had shed their stiffness. Feeling quite at ease, they were participating in the exchanges.

After twenty minutes or so, when the snacks were exhausted, Ram-babu lit a cigar; offering Bhupesh-babu a cigarette, Byomkesh then held the tin out to Banamali-babu. 'One for you, Banabehari-babu?' he said.

'I don't smoke . . .' said Banamali-babu, and turned pale. 'Er . . . my name . . .'

'The two of you are brothers, and I know your real

names—Rashbehari and Banabehari Biswas.' Byomkesh sat down in his chair. 'Natabar Nashkar was blackmailing you. You were paying him eighty rupees a month . . .'

Rashbehari and Banabehari had turned to blocks of wood. Lighting his own cigarette, Byomkesh spoke as he blew the smoke out, 'Natabar Nashkar was a devil. When he was in Dhaka, he was to all appearances an agent, but behind that façade he was a blackmailer whenever he had the opportunity. When the two of you went to jail, he procured a copy of the court judgement, keeping future possibilities in mind. His plan was to wait till you had got jobs again after your release and then start sucking your blood.

'Then the Partition took place. Natabar could no longer continue his business in Dhaka, he escaped to Calcutta. But he did not know too many people here; there was no opportunity to pursue either his legal or his illegal profession as there was no one suitable for blackmailing. His business reached a low ebb. He took a room in this boarding house, surviving on whatever little money he had managed to bring.

'While he was here, he suddenly saw the two of you one day and recognized you. You lived in the same boarding house. On making enquiries, he discovered that you were working at a bank under false identities. Natabar Nashkar found a channel for earning. God seemed to have trussed up the two of you and delivered you to him.

'Pay up, or else I will reveal your real identities to the bank, Natabar told you. Helpless, you began paying him every month. Not a large sum, admittedly, only eighty rupees. But not bad for Natabar—at least it paid for his accommodation and food.

'So it went on. The two of you had no peace, nor could you escape Natabar's clutches. Your only hope lay in his death.'

Byomkesh paused. Breaking the breathless silence, Banabehari burst out, 'I beg of you Byomkesh-babu, we didn't kill Natabar Nashkar. We were in Bhupesh-babu's room when he was killed.'

'That is true.' Leaning back in his chair, Byomkesh said carelessly, 'I do not care who killed Natabar. Only the police do. But the two of you work at a bank. If there is ever a discrepancy in the accounts I shall be forced to reveal your true identities.'

'There will be no discrepancy in the bank's accounts,' Ram-babu aka Rashbehari-babu finally spoke. 'We will not repeat our mistake.'

'Excellent. Ajit and I shall remain silent in that case.' Byomkesh looked at Bhupesh-babu. 'What about you?'

A strange smile flitted across Bhupesh-babu's face. 'I shall remain silent too,' he said softly. 'Not a word shall escape my lips.'

The room was silent for some time after this. Then Ram-babu rose, speaking with his palms joined together, 'We shall never forget your generosity. May we leave now? I am not feeling very well.'

'You may.' Byomkesh saw them to the door, then came back after shutting it.

I saw Bhupesh-babu smiling at Byomkesh. Byomkesh returned his smile. 'I did not know there was an illicit connection between Natabar Nashkar and Ram-babu and Banamali-babu. That is a coincidence. You have probably unravelled everything, have you not?'

'Not everything, but the sum of it,' Byomkesh sighed deeply.

'Why don't you tell the story? If I have anything to add I shall do so afterwards.'

Giving Bhupesh-babu a cigarette and lighting one for himself, Byomkesh looked at me and began to speak, slowly. 'You wrote an account of Natabar's death. When I read it, I was struck by a doubt. The sound of a pistol being fired is never so loud. This seemed to be the sound of a shotgun, or a bomb bursting. Yet Natabar had been killed by a pistol shot.

'You had noticed the similarity in appearance between Ram-babu and Banamali-babu. When I spoke to them, they appeared to be concealing something. Since they used to frequent Natabar's room, I became curious about them.

'But they were in Bhupesh-babu's room on the first floor when the gunshot was heard. The atmosphere in Bhupesh-babu's room was peaceful, normal. He was in his own room; at 6.25 Rashbehari and Banabehari came for the game of bridge. But the game could not begin till Ajit had arrived. A couple of minutes later Ajit's sandals were heard flapping on the stairs. Bhupesh-babu rose and opened the window looking out on the lane. At once there was an explosion. Rashbehari and Banabehari went up to the window. "There . . . there . . . he ran out of the lane just this minute, did you see him? He had a brown shawl on . . ." Bhupesh-babu exclaimed.

'There were several people walking past the lane on the main road. Rashbehari and Banabehari assumed one of them had just run out of the lane. They were left in no doubt that Bhupesh-babu was right. It is possible to induce such mistakes if you want to.

'Later the pistol was found on the window sill of Natabar's room. Naturally the question arises, why had the assailant left the pistol behind? There was no justifiable reason. I suspected that there was serious deception at work behind this apparently simple occurrence.

'Haripada, the servant, had heard someone in Natabar's room at six in the evening. What if that person had killed Natabar? And had then pushed back the supposed time of the killing in order to create an alibi for himself? A difference of fifteen minutes in the time of death cannot be detected by a postmortem.

'I was convinced that the murderer was not an outsider, but someone who lived in the boarding house. But who was it? Was it Shibkali-babu? Rashebhari and Banabehari? Or someone else? I did not know who had a motive, but only Shibkali-babu had the opportunity. Everyone else had a watertight alibi.

'My mind was fogged; I could not see anything clearly. I had noticed that Natabar's room was directly beneath

Bhupesh-babu's, and Natabar-babu's window was directly beneath Bhupesh-babu's. But the thought of a cracker hadn't even occurred to me then. Yes, a cracker. The kind that explodes when hurled, or when it is dropped from a height on a hard surface.

'I was on my way to the police station this morning in the hope of some fresh information. As I was leaving, I thought of checking for clues in the lane near Natabar's window.

'I did find a clue. The discoloured stain left behind by a cracker which burst on the paved surface of the lane directly beneath Natabar's window. When I sniffed it I discovered a faint tang of gunpowder. All my doubts were now dispelled. An excellent alibi had been created. Who had created the alibi? It could not have been anyone except Bhupesh-babu. Because he was the one who had opened the window. Rashbehari and Banabehari had gone up to the window after hearing the bang.

'Bhupesh-babu went downstairs quietly at six that evening under cover of darkness. The pistol had already been procured; he entered Natabar's room, introduced himself and shot him. Opening the window looking out on the lane, he placed the pistol on the window sill and returned to his room. Fortunately no one saw him on his journey to and from Natabar's room. But just in case they had, he needed an alibi. Returning to his room, he waited. Rashbehari and Banabehari arrived in ten minutes for their game of bridge. But Ajit had not arrived yet, so the three of them waited for him.

'Then Bhupesh-babu heard Ajit's sandals flapping on the staircase. He was prepared, holding a marble-sized cracker in his clenched hand. On the pretext of stuffiness in the room, he opened the window looking out on the lane and dropped the cracker. There was a bang downstairs. Rashbehari and Banabehari rushed to the window; Bhupesh-babu showed them the imaginary murderer in the brown shawl.

'Bhupesh-babu did not have to do anything more; the corpse was discovered in due course. The police came and took the corpse away. Curtain.'

Byomkesh stopped. Bhupesh-babu had been listening without a word, without stirring, he remained the same way. 'Any errors?' Byomkesh asked him, arching his eyebrows.

Bhupesh-babu stirred now, shaking his head with a smile. 'None whatsoever. I was the one who made the error. I didn't imagine you'd be back so soon, Byomkesh-babu. I had expected Natabar's case to have died down by the time you returned.'

'Two questions remain unanswered,' Byomkesh smiled. 'First, what was your motive? Second, how did you muffle the sound of the pistol being fired? Even if you fire a pistol in a closed room, the sound is likely to be heard outside. Did you take no care to prevent this?'

'I shall answer the second question first.' Removing the shawl folded over his shoulder, he unfolded it and held it out before us with both his hands; we saw a small hole in the new shawl. 'I was dressed in this shawl when I went to Natabar's room, hiding the pistol under it. I shot Natabar without taking the pistol out of my shawl; the sound was muffled by it, no one heard.'

Byomkesh nodded slowly. 'And the answer to my first question?' he said. 'I can guess some of it; you had shown us your son's photograph yesterday. Still, I want to hear it from you.'

A pulse began to beat in Bhupesh-babu's forehead, but he spoke calmly. 'I had shown you my son's photograph because I realized you would discover the truth. So I was justifying myself in advance. Natabar tricked my son into accompanying him from school on the day the riots broke out in Dhaka. That evening he came to my house to tell me he would return my son for a ransom of ten thousand rupees. I did not have ten thousand in cash, I gave him whatever I had; my wife took off all her jewellery and handed it to him. Natabar left with all of it, but we did not get our son back. We did not see Natabar either. Several years had passed since then. When I came to Calcutta after losing my wife and son, one day I suddenly spotted Natabar on the road. And then . . .'

'I see,' said Byomkesh. 'There is no need to say anything more, Bhupesh-babu.'

Bhupesh-babu remained immobile for a few moments. Then he said, 'What do you wish to do with me?'

Byomkesh looked at the ceiling for a while. Then he said, '"No one hangs for killing a crow," the writer Sarat Chandra Chattopadhyay had said. I believe no one should hang for killing a vulture either. You need not worry.'

Byomkesh and Barada

1

It wasn't so very long ago that Barada-babu, the ghost-seeker, had run into Byomkesh, the truth-seeker. Byomkesh was by nature opposed to the outdoors; he preferred to spin his spider's web in a corner of the room. But on that occasion he had surprised everyone with a journey of three hundred miles.

A childhood friend of Byomkesh's was employed as Deputy Superintendent of Police in the state of Bihar. He had been transferred to Munger some time earlier and had begun to hurl letters at Byomkesh at regular intervals. There must have been a hidden motive behind his cordial invitations; for the mind refuses to imagine that a DSP would want to revive an ancient, half-forgotten friendship without any reason.

It was the middle of September; the clouds had lost

their colour, perhaps due to their excessive extravagance. On a day such as this Byomkesh suggested with a kind of desperation on receiving a letter from his policeman friend, 'Let us visit Munger.'

I was ready. There's something in the autumn air before Durga Puja that relentlessly pushes the resident Bengali away from home and the non-resident Bengali, towards it. 'Let's,' I said happily.

Arriving at Munger at the appointed hour, we discovered the DSP waiting for us. His name was Shashanka-babu. Probably the same age as ourselves, he had not yet crossed his thirties; yet his expression and behaviour had already acquired an air of middle-aged gravity. It seemed he had aged under the weight of additional responsibilities thrust on upon him while still relatively young. He took us to his official quarters inside the fort and settled us in.

The part of Munger referred to as 'fort' retains none of its fortitude; but once upon a time it had in fact been Mir Kasim's impregnable fort. It was a circular area with a perimeter of almost a quarter of a mile, surrounded by ramparts and a moat, with the Ganga flowing on the left. There were only three exit gates. At present the fort held—besides the living quarters for high-ranking state and judicial officials, the jail, and an extensive playground—the residences of a handful of ordinary citizens too. The town, the market and actual human habitation were outside; the fort was seemingly a sovereign, upper-class enclave for royals and noblemen.

I became acquainted with Shashanka-babu at his residence over breakfast and a cup of tea. He welcomed us profusely; but I observed that the man was exceedingly cunning, considerably adept at conversation. Unless you paid close attention, you would not realize how he had unobtrusively got to the point during seemingly aimless chatter about memories of old friendship and a list of sights worth seeing in Munger. At least, there was no doubt that he was a man of action, bringing up the real issue with such verbal finesse that there could be no scope for resentment or dissatisfaction.

As a matter of fact I had not even grasped that he had raised the real issue within half an hour of our reaching his residence; but a hint of amusement in Byomkesh's eyes alerted me. 'I shall not disappoint you with sights like historic ruins or hot water springs alone,' Shashanka-babu was saying at the time. 'If you are interested in the supernatural, I can show you something of that too. A mysterious ghost has arrived in our town lately—I am somewhat perturbed by him.'

'Are you normally perturbed by ghosts in your line of duty?' asked Byomkesh.

'Not at all,' Shashanka-babu smiled. 'But the way things have turned out . . . The thing is, a gentleman died rather mysteriously in this very fort about six months ago. The mystery of his death has not been solved yet, but his spirit has already started haunting the house he lived in.'

Byomkesh put down his empty cup; I observed deep

amusement playing in his eyes. Wiping his mouth carefully with a handkerchief, he drawled, 'Shashanka, I can see your conversational skills are as strong as ever—constant application has refined it further. It has been less than an hour since we set foot in Munger, yet I am already drawn to your local drama by the description you gave. Give me all the details.'

A meeting of true minds. Grasping what Byomkesh was hinting at, Shashanka-babu may have been slightly embarrassed. But his expression betrayed none of this. 'Another cup of tea?' he said casually. 'No? Some paan? Here you are, Ajit-babu. All right, let me recount the incident; although it is not particularly spine-tingling. It took place six months ago . . .'

Popping some paan into his mouth, Shashanka-babu began his story.

'There is a particular house in the fort, near the southern gate. Although small, it is two-storied, with a clearing around it. The houses inside the fort are all at some distance from each other; not as congested as the houses in cities. Every house has its own compound. The owner of this house is a rich local nobleman—he rents it out.

'This man who had occupied the house for the past fifteen years was named Baikuntha Das. He was getting on in years—a goldsmith by caste. He had a gold-and-silver shop in the market, but that was only for show. His real business was with jewels. His account books showed that he had fifty-one precious jewels in his possession when he died—diamonds, pearls, rubies and emeralds whose value amounted to some two-and-a-half lakh rupees.

'He used to keep all these precious jewels at home and not in his shop. And yet the strange thing was that he did not even have an iron safe at home. No one knows where he stashed his precious jewels. When a customer came he would take him home, and then, giving him a seat in the drawing room, he would go upstairs to fetch the jewels from his bedroom to display them.

'You can understand from the extent of his riches that he was a wealthy man. But no one would suspect as much from his appearance. Rather a harmless middle-aged man, extraordinarily devoted to the gods, a holy necklace of tulsi leaves draped around his neck—his palms were permanently joined in supplication. But were anyone to approach him for a donation for a good cause, he would sink into such gloom and despair that the local young men had stopped asking him for contributions. His name too had been distorted in the process; he was laughingly called Miser, rather than Mister, Baikuntha. The entire Bengali population of the town referred to him as Miser Goldsmith.

'The man was indeed uncommonly parsimonious. His monthly expenses ran to seventy rupees, forty out of which was his rent. He paid for his own, his daughter's and an idiot servant's food and clothing with the remaining thirty rupees. I have seen his accounts book; his expenses never crossed seventy rupees. Unusual, is it not? I used to wonder why a miser like him paid such a high rent to live inside the fort. He could have lived outside on a far lower rent.'

Byomkesh was lying back in his deck chair, his eyes on the entrance to the none-too-distant fort of stone. 'The interiors of the fort must be safer, with fewer thieves or robbers,' he observed. 'Someone in possession of two-and-a-half lakh rupees' worth of jewels is bound to seek a residence in a secure area. Mister Baikuntha may have been a miser but he was probably not careless.'

'I assumed as much,' responded Shashanka-babu. 'But as the story reveals, he could not escape the eagle eyes of thieves despite the security offered by the fort. The theft must have been planned quite some time earlier. Munger may be a small town, but do not dismiss it as inconsequential.'

'Of course not, why would I do that,' protested Byomkesh.

'There are a couple of great souls here whose skills at theft, shooting and murder even your Calcutta might be hard put to match. What can I tell you, even the government is concerned about them. You know there are many gun-foundries here dating back to Mir Kasim's time, don't you? But never mind all that now; let me first tell you the tale of Baikuntha the goldsmith.'

Having used these slightly irrelevant details to drop significant hints about the vital responsibilities borne by the police and himself, he continued . . .

'On the 26th of April, Baikuntha-babu returned home from his shop at eight in the evening. He was a simple man, with no premonition of the imminent mishap.

After dinner, he went to sleep in his first-floor room at approximately nine o' clock. His daughter used to sleep in the prayer room downstairs. After giving her father his meal, she went to her room and locked the door. The idiot servant used to guard the shop at night; he left as soon as the owner returned. Nobody knows what happened in the house after that.

'When Baikuntha-babu didn't emerge in the morning, the door was broken down. The police found his corpse on the floor in a sitting position, its back against the wall. There were no injuries—the assailant had strangled him to death, and then escaped with all his jewels.'

'So the murderer entered through the open window?' asked Byomkesh.

'So it seems,' answered Shashanka-babu. 'Since the only door to the room was locked, there was no other way in besides the window! I suspect Baikuntha-babu went to sleep with the window open; it was summer—and a particularly hot night. There were no bars on the window, which made it simple for the thieves to climb into the room using a ladder.'

'All of Baikuntha-babu's jewels were stolen?'

'All of them. Jewels worth two-and-a-half lakh rupees gone. Not a single one was found. The thieves didn't spare the money in his personal wooden case either, they took everything.'

'Did Baikuntha-babu keep his jewels in this case?'

'Where else could he have kept them? Of course,

there's no proof that he did. No one was allowed into his bedroom; not even his daughter knew their whereabouts. But as I told you already, his room didn't even have a safe; and yet he used to keep all the diamonds and pearls and all else in his bedroom. So it must be assumed he kept them in the case.'

'Was there no other box or case in the room?'

'Nothing at all. You will be amazed to know the room held nothing but a mat, a pillow, that case, another case for his paan, and a pitcher of water. Not even a picture on the wall.'

'A paan-case. You did examine it carefully?' asked Byomkesh.

Shashanka-babu offered an unhappy smile. 'Look, we're not as stupid as you think we are. We went through everything in the room with a fine-tooth comb. The paan-case had a hunk of lime and some of the things that go into a paan, including the leaves. The case was made of brass, with separate compartments for each of the ingredients. Baikuntha-babu was addicted to paan—and because he didn't like the way others made it, he prepared his own paan. Is there any other information you need?'

'Oh no, this is sufficient,' responded Byomkesh with a laugh. 'There is no doubting the patience and application of the police; everyone agrees there. If only they were accompanied by a little intelligence . . . but never mind all that. The long and short of it is that one or more thieves murdered Baikuntha-babu and fled with jewels worth two-

and-a-half-lakh rupees. Have you heard whether there have been attempts to sell the jewels anywhere?'

'The jewels have not been put up for sale yet. We would have heard if they had been. We have observers everywhere.'

'Very well. And then?'

'That's as far as it goes. Baikuntha-babu's daughter is in a sorry state. He did not leave any money behind; there wasn't a single rupee to be found anywhere. All she has is the little money she got by selling the gold and silver in the shop. It is distressing to see a Bengali girl from a respectable family being forced to be a dependant of someone else in a foreign land because of poverty.'

'Whom is she a dependant of?'

'A veteran lawyer from hereabouts—his name is Tarashankar-babu. He has volunteered to have the daughter stay in his house. You have to say he's a decent sort despite being a lawyer. He was on good terms with Baikuntha-babu—they used to play chess every Sunday afternoon . . .'

'Hmm. Is the girl a widow?'

'No, she's married. But it wouldn't be incorrect to call her a widow. She was married young, her husband soon became wayward. A drunkard and a debauch, he used to act on stage till he suddenly left with a circus troupe. He has been missing since then. That was why Baikuntha-babu had got his daughter to live with him.'

'How old is she?'

'About twenty-three or twenty-four.'

'Character?'

'Upright, so far as I know. Her appearance also favours morality—you could describe her as a veritable hag. The poor husband cannot really be blamed . . .'

'I see. No family anywhere?'

'None to speak of. Her father's younger brother's sons live in Nabadwip. Some of them rushed here when they heard. But when they saw there was not a drop of juice left, that the thieves had taken everything, they peeled off one by one.'

Byomkesh was silent for several minutes; then he said, exhaling, 'Quite a novel affair. But it is probably too late to do anything about it now. Besides, I am a visitor, here today gone tomorrow. I should not interfere with your work. You will probably not approve either.'

'Oh no, why should you interfere?' declared Shashanka-babu. 'I'm not making an official request to you; but you're a fellow-traveller, if your observations lead you to certain ideas you can always help me personally. You're here on holiday; I do not wish to burden you with responsibilities.'

Shashanka-babu's intentions were plain now. He was more than willing to accept help, but he was unwilling to 'offically' give anyone else the credit and thus share the fame.

'Very well, so be it,' Byomkesh smiled too. 'I shall help you without taking the formal responsibility. By the way, what was that you were saying about the house being ghost-infested?'

'Another tenant, also a Bengali, moved into the house some time after Baikuntha-babu's death,' explained Shashanka-babu. 'Ever since his arrival, the nuisance of ghosts has begun. Not everything can be believed, of course, but uncanny things have taken place. A fifteen-foot tall spirit peeps in through the window at night. Some other people besides the tenant have seen it too.'

'What!'

'Yes. There's a gentleman named Barada-babu here . . . Oh, talk of the devil. Here he is. And Shailen-babu too. Wonderful. Do come in. Byomkesh, Barada-babu is an expert in the supernatural. You can listen to the ghostly tale directly from him.'

2

After preliminary pleasantries, both of them took their seats. Barada-babu was rotund, diminutive, fair of skin and clean-shaven. All told, he reminded one of fresh potatoes. His companion Shailen-babu was just the opposite; tall and thin, though you could not call him frail. We learnt more about them in the course of our conversation. Barada-babu was a local resident, earning a living from inherited property and subsidiary ownership rights to a few houses, and dabbling in the supernatural in his spare time. Shailen-babu was a wealthy man who had come to Munger to recover his health—but the place suited his physical disposition so well that he had decided to purchase a house and reside here permanently. Neither was over forty years of age.

We introduced ourselves as well—but it turned out that they had never even heard of Byomkesh. Such is fame.

Be that as it may, after the introductions Barada-babu said, 'You were being regaled with the tale of Miser Baikuntha, were you not? Tragic affair—an unnatural death. I am convinced that his soul shall not find release unless the last rites are performed at Gaya.'

Byomkesh stirred. 'Do you not believe in spirits and the afterlife?' asked Barada-babu with a sharp glance in his direction.

'I do not disbelieve them either,' Byomkesh smiled. 'They are outside my calculations.'

'Even if you wish to keep them outside your calculations, they refuse to be kept out,' Barada-babu responded. 'That is where the problem lies. You did not believe in ghosts and spirits either, Shailen-babu; you used to laugh them off as a hoax. But now?'

'It would not be an exaggeration to say I have blind faith in them now,' Barada-babu's companion said. 'Indeed, Byomkesh-babu, I was like you once. I never bothered about ghosts. But after becoming acquainted with Barada-babu here, the more we discuss the subject the more convinced I am that living in this world without taking spirits into consideration is more or less impossible.'

'I don't know,' replied Byomkesh. 'Speaking for ourselves, we seem to be surviving quite well without them. And besides, people's lives are already becoming so complicated that to add . . .'

'Never mind all that,' Shashanka-babu interrupted. 'Barada-babu, why don't you tell Byomkesh-babu that ghost story of Baikuntha-babu's?'

'Yes, that's a splendid idea,' said Byomkesh. 'Stories are far more entertaining than theory.'

A flash of satisfaction appeared on Barada-babu's countenance. There are many people in the world who want to tell stories—but not all of them are fortunate enough to have attentive listeners. Most individuals are sceptical, looking for holes to pick, more intent on arguing than on listening. Therefore, Barada-babu cheered up as though he had received an unexpected gift when Byomkesh acquiesced to a story instead of theory. I realized that he had not been fortunate enough to secure a courteous and patient listener very often.

Not everyone tells stories the same way; Barada-babu's style was quite attractive. He did not rush through his tale—it proceeded at a stately pace; the narration was not marred by an abundance of incidents, but the events were woven together with such expertise that the listener's attention was gradually subjugated. The expressions on his face and in his eyes accompanied the story so perfectly that the experience was a fulfilling one.

'You have heard of Baikuntha-babu's death. An unnatural death; he had no opportunity to prepare for the afterlife. We believe that when a soul is unexpectedly separated from the body, its attachment to the body is not extinguished—in other words, it is not even able to comprehend that it no longer belongs to a corporeal body. In other cases, even if it does comprehend, it cannot overcome its attachment to the physical world; it continues to haunt the spaces that it was accustomed to inhabiting when alive.

'I am not asking you to subscribe to these theories. But the supernatural story that I am about to recount cannot be explained satisfactorily in any other manner. The veracity of the events is beyond question. I have a reputation for telling fantastical tales; but in this case even the most diehard sceptic has been compelled to acknowledge that there is not an iota of exaggeration in my story. Do you agree, Shailen-babu?'

'Yes,' confirmed Shailen-babu. 'Even Amalya-babu had no choice but to admit that the events were not fabricated.'

'Therefore,' continued Barada-babu, 'whatever the reasons might be, that these things took place is beyond doubt. Baikuntha-babu's house remained under the control of the police for a few weeks after his death; meanwhile, Tarashankar-babu put Baikuntha-babu's daughter up at his own house. I cannot say whether any incidents took place during this period, for the two police constables who had been stationed to guard the house probably used to sleep too soundly at night after a couple of drinks to be in any condition to observe the arrival of incorporeal creatures like ghosts and spirits. Anyway, once the police had withdrawn from the house, a new tenant arrived. His name was Kailashchandra Mallik—he's quite ill and getting on in years. He came to Munger to recover his health and, without making any enquiries, he took possession of the first available house he found within the fort. The owner of the house did not display any anxiety to disclose that a murder had taken place here.

'A few days did pass uneventfully. Kailashbabu occupied the solitary bedroom on the first floor—the one in which Baikuntha-babu had been murdered. His servant and cook lived on the ground floor. A rural landowner, Kailash-babu was reasonably affluent. He was engaged in a dispute with his only son, his wife was no longer alive either—hence he was solely dependent on his servant and cook during this journey for a change of air.

'After a week had passed, the ghost arrived. As he was preparing to sleep at about nine in the evening, after he had taken his pills, his eyes drifted towards the window. Since it was summer, the window was open—he discovered a repulsively ugly face peering at him. Kailash-babu screamed, whereupon his servant and cook both ran upstairs. But the face had disappeared by then.

'The same incident was repeated on two other nights. Everyone had tried to dismiss the first occurrence as the product of Kailash-babu's fevered imagination, but they could no longer persist with this argument now. The news spread. Although we had not been acquainted with Kailash-babu yet, the news came to us as well.

'I have a scientific interest in ghosts and spirits. I can neither dismiss them as non-existent, nor accept their existence unquestioningly. Therefore, while others rejoiced in the possibility of using the series of incidents as a juicy opportunity for ridicule, I decided to examine it further; just because it was unnatural it did not necessarily have to be untrue.

'One day, a few friends and I called on Kailash-babu. Crippled by his illness—a bad heart—he had been forbidden by the doctor to come downstairs; he summoned us to his bedroom. Despite an irritable temperament, his manners were impeccable—he welcomed us with due ceremony and provided us with an authentic account of his supernatural encounter.

'The spirit had appeared on four occasions in the past fortnight, he said. On all four occasions it had peered through the window—and then vanished. There was no fixed hour of arrival—it appeared in the middle of the night, in the early hours of the morning, and even in the evening. Its appearance was far from pleasant, its eyes radiating greed and hunger. As though it wished to enter the room, but was being forced to retreat by the presence of a human.

'Kailash-babu's tale convinced us that we had to witness this for ourselves. He extended a warm invitation to us. We began to patrol his bedroom every day thereafter. From sunset till ten at night—sometimes beyond eleven. But there was no sign of the spectre. Even when it did make a rare appearance, it was always after our departure; we never set eyes on it.

'After ten days of this, my friends stopped coming one by one; even Shailen-babu gave up. I was the only one to continue. I would arrive after sunset, converse with Kailash-babu all evening, and leave at about ten-thirty or eleven.

'Another week passed in this manner. I began to lose hope too. What kind of a spirit was this that could not be seen by anyone other than Kailash-babu? I began to harbour other suspicions about him.

'Then, suddenly, I was rewarded for my diligence. My doubts about Kailash-babu dissipated too.'

'You saw the spirit for yourself?' asked Byomkesh, who had been listening intently.

'Yes, I did,' answered Barada-babu solemnly.

'Of course,' said Byomkesh, leaning back in his chair. Then he asked after some thought, 'Did you recognize Baikuntha-babu?'

'I cannot say I did,' Barada-babu shook his head. 'It was a face, not very clear—but undoubtedly human. It appeared dimly for a few moments before disappearing.'

'Quite extraordinary,' remarked Byomkesh. 'Not many people are fortunate enough to have seen a ghost with their own eyes; in most cases, analysing the supernatural encounter reveals that it was either hearsay or a case of mistaken identity.'

The palpable trace of scepticism in Byomkesh's statement seemed to cut Shailen-babu to the quick; 'It wasn't just Barada-babu,' he said, 'many others saw it too after that.'

'Even you?' asked Byomkesh.

'Yes, so did I,' he responded. 'Perhaps not as clearly as Barada-babu, but still I did see it. After Barada-babu had seen the face, some of us had begun to visit Kailash-babu again. One day I succeeded in catching a glimpse for an instant.'

'In his excitement Shailen-babu made a small error, which was why he was unable to see it properly,' explained Barada-babu. 'Some of us—Amulya, Dr Sachi Roy and I—were talking to Kailash-babu. We had become somewhat distracted in the course of advising him to leave the house, but Shailen-babu had his eyes trained on the window like a hunter. Suddenly he shouted out "There, there . . ." All of us turned towards the window at once, but nothing more could be seen. Shailen-babu had seen a cloud of vapour gradually assuming a shape. But he had called out before it could materialize completely, which was why it disappeared.'

'Still, Kailash-babu must have seen it too,' Shailen-babu said. 'Don't you remember him losing consciousness?'

'Yes, his heart was already weak,' responded Barada-babu. Fortunately Dr Roy was present; he gave him an injection at once and brought him back to his senses. Otherwise another tragedy could have occurred.'

After this we sat in silence for a few minutes. It was impossible not to believe eyewitness statements. Unless we were ready to consider at least two respectable gentlemen out-and-out liars, we would have to assume that they were telling the truth. And yet, their story was so unusual that we did not feel inclined to accept it unquestioningly.

Eventually Byomkesh said, 'In your opinion, therefore, it is Baikuntha-babu's spirit that is appearing at the window of his bedroom.'

‘What else can it possibly be?’ asked Barada-babu.

‘What is Baikuntha-babu’s daughter’s viewpoint on this?’

‘Her viewpoint is not easy to ascertain. I had suggested performing the last rites in Gaya, but she did nothing about it. Tarashankar-babu in particular pays no heed to such suggestions—he laughs them away.’ Barada-babu emitted a regretful sigh.

‘Perhaps Baikuntha-babu’s soul would find release were the mystery of his murder to be unravelled. I know nothing about the supernatural; but still, if there is such a thing as an afterlife, it would not be unnatural for spirits to harbour a proclivity for revenge,’ said Byomkesh.

‘Of course it would not be unnatural,’ agreed Barada-babu. ‘The spirit only lacks a corporeal body, but its soul is intact. As the Gita says, *nainangchhidantishastrani* . . . Weapons do not harm it, fire does not burn it . . .’

‘Can you introduce me to Baikuntha-babu’s daughter?’ interrupted Byomkesh. ‘I would like to ask her a couple of questions.’

‘I can try,’ said Barada-babu after a few minutes’ thought. ‘Perhaps Tarashankar-babu will not object when he hears you’re a detective. I shall meet him at the bar library today; if he agrees, I will accompany you to his house in the evening. That’s settled, then.’

When I realized he was about to leave, I asked Barada-babu, ‘Can we not see the ghost too?’

‘I cannot promise you an instant glimpse,’ he replied, ‘but

if you display diligence and determination, you will surely see it. Why don't we visit Kailash-babu this evening directly after meeting Tarashankar-babu? Well, Byomkesh-babu?'

'Excellent proposal. I am particularly keen. I would love to return from your city with a new experience.'

'Then I shall take my leave now. It is ten o' clock. I shall be back at about five in the evening.'

After Barada-babu and Shailen-babu had left, Shashanka-babu asked, 'What do you think? Extraordinary, is it not?'

'I cannot tell which one is more absurd—your murder story or Barada-babu's ghost story.'

'What was so absurd about my murder story?'

'How else should I describe a murder that cannot be solved even in six months? Are you sure Baikuntha-babu was murdered? He did not have a heart attack, did he?'

'What do you mean? The doctor's postmortem report clearly said he was strangled to death. There were subcutaneous abrasions on this throat . . .'

'And yet the murderer had left no sign, not even a fingerprint. To call it absurd is putting it mildly. Barada-babu at least has a ghost he saw himself, you don't even have that.' Rising to his feet, Byomkesh said, stretching, 'Up, Ajit, let us have our baths. I didn't sleep a wink on the train; I cannot be myself without a peaceful afternoon nap.'

3

Barada-babu arrived in the evening. Tarashankar-babu had acquiesced; although he was rather unfavourably disposed towards such unnecessary intrusions into the life of a grieving lady.

We left with Barada-babu. Shashanka-babu was unable to accompany us, as he had suddenly been summoned by a senior officer.

Barada-babu informed us on the way that Tarashankar-babu was not a bad sort, and that no other lawyer in the district could match him on sharpness of intellect. Even the judges feared his incisive and bitter tongue. We were unlikely to receive a warm welcome from him, but we should not take that to heart.

Byomkesh smiled in response. He was as thick-skinned as an elephant when he was pursuing his own objective—no one could humiliate him. Consorting with him was thickening my own hide too.

Exiting through the southern gate of the fort, we arrived at a locality named Balloonbazar. It was dominated by Bengalis, with Tarashankar-babu's palatial residence situated at its centre. We were left in no doubt that Tarashankar-babu was a sharp-witted lawyer.

Entering his drawing room, we found a bedstead covered with a sheet, on which sat the householder, leaning back against a pillow and smoking a hookah. Tall and thin, his body lacked flesh rather than possessing an excess of it; his face was angular and his gaze, piercing. His age was approaching sixty; his attire comprised a dhoti and a white scarf for the upper part of his body. He sat up at our arrival, holding the pipe of his hookah in one hand, and said, 'Do come in, Barada. These are the detectives from Calcutta, I take it?'

His voice and manner of speaking held a quality that disconcerted listeners. Possibly this was the sign of a successful lawyer; it was not difficult to imagine witnesses on the other side becoming positively panic-stricken.

Barada-babu introduced Byomkesh diffidently. 'I am a seeker of truth,' said Byomkesh, greeting him courteously.

Arching his left eyebrow upward a little, Tarashankar-babu enquired, 'Seeker of truth? And what might that be?'

'Seeking the truth is my profession—just as the law is yours,' answered Byomkesh.

Tarashankar-babu's lips curled in a sarcastic smile. 'I see—the word detective is no longer in fashion then? What is it that you seek?'

'The truth.'

'I heard you say that already. What kind of truth?'

'For instance, how much money Baikuntha-babu had left with you,' Byomkesh responded in a measured tone. 'Learning truths such as these will do for now.'

Every sign of sarcasm and mockery was wiped off Tarashankar-babu's expression at once. He stared at Byomkesh, his eyes practically popping out. 'How did you know Baikuntha had left some money with me?' he asked in utter consternation.

'I am a seeker of truth,' answered Byomkesh.

Tarashankar-babu was speechless for a minute. When he spoke again, his tone was transformed; 'Extraordinary!'

he declared with a mixture of reverence and admiration. 'I have not been witness to such an ability ever before. Please take a seat, pray do not keep standing. Do sit down, Barada. Does Byomkesh-babu also have a pet ghost like you?'

After we had taken our seats, Tarshankar-babu took a few quick puffs on his hookah before raising his head again. Looking at Byomkesh, he said, 'I realize now you were merely hazarding a guess. But how did you happen to make such a guess? Even an assumption needs some ingredients.'

'But there were plenty of ingredients,' Byomkesh laughed. 'Can anyone believe that a wealthy businessman like Baikuntha-babu would leave behind no cash? And yet there was no money in his bank account. He was probably suspicious of institutions like banks. Then where did he keep his money? Almost certainly with a trusted friend. Baikuntha-babu used to visit you every Sunday afternoon to play chess. You have taken his daughter under your wing after his death; therefore one must conclude that you were his most trusted and most trustworthy friend.'

'Your surmise is correct,' agreed Tarashankar-babu. 'Baikuntha had no faith in banks. All his cash was always kept with me, as it still is. It is not a small sum of money, some seventeen thousand rupees. But I have not revealed the existence of this money; I did not wish to have it known after his death. But since Byomkesh-babu has discovered the truth I have no choice but to admit it. Still, I would prefer that this not be revealed to anyone else.

The three of you know, but no one else should. Do you follow me, Barada?'

Barada-babu nodded, his doubt reflected on his face.

'Is there any particular reason to keep this a secret?' asked Byomkesh.

After a few more puffs on his hookah, Tarashankar-babu said, 'There is. You may suspect I am trying to appropriate the money that my friend had deposited in my safekeeping—I don't care a jot about that. There is a different reason for not revealing it.'

'May I know what that other reason is?'

Knitting his brows, Tarashankar-babu pondered on the subject for a while. Then, after a quick glance at the curtained door leading into the house, he said, lowering his voice, 'You are probably not aware that Baikuntha had a scoundrel as a son-in-law. Instead of giving a home to his wife, he travels the country with a circus troupe. I have no idea of his whereabouts at present, but if he were to discover by some means that his wife has come into a great deal of money, he will take her away by force. After squandering the money in a matter of days, he will vanish again. I do not want that to happen, you see.'

'I see,' Byomkesh responded slowly, his eyes on the sheet.

'Everything that Baikuntha had has been stolen already,' Tarashankar-babu continued. 'All that remains are these few thousand rupees. If Mr Son-in-Law turns up to fritter away these as well, what will the poor, ill-fated girl be left with? What will she survive on the rest of her life? I won't be alive forever, after all.'

'You are right,' said Byomkesh, who had been listening with his face resting on his palm. 'I would like to ask her a few questions. She is at home, is she not? If it is not too much of a bother . . .'

'Very well. I don't think interrogating her will help. But since you want to, I shall fetch her here.'

When he had left, I asked Byomkesh a question with my eyes and eyebrows—to which he responded with a faint smile. Since he might not want to talk openly in Baradababu's presence, I could not ask him anything directly. I began to wonder what kind of a man Tarashankarbabu was . . .

He returned five minutes later; trailing behind him, a young woman stood in silence at the door. Her head was only half-covered with the end of her sari, which offered no impediment to a view of her face; she was dressed like an everyday married woman. Even if she did not exactly resemble a witch who had risen from the swamp, she could by no means be termed beautiful. Still, possibly the greatest flaw in her appearance was the complete lack of expression on her face. It was doubtful whether another face so expressionless could be seen outside China and Japan. The lifelessness in her features had made her lack of beauty even more prominent. During the entire time she stood before us, not a muscle twitched on her face, not once did she raise her eyes from the floor. Offering the briefest of answers to Byomkesh's question in a dull voice, without any play of emotions on her face, she vanished behind the curtain like a mechanical figure.

As soon as she arrived, Byomkesh turned towards her swiftly, surveying her from head to toe before speaking calmly. 'You are probably aware of the fact that you have not been entirely bankrupted by your father's death.'

'Yes.'

'Tarashankar-babu must have informed you that seventeen thousand rupees belonging to you is in his safekeeping.'

'Yes.'

Byomkesh seemed a little disappointed. He continued after a little thought, 'How long has your husband been missing?'

'Eight years.'

'You have not seen him at all in this period?'

'No.'

'Nor received a single letter from him?'

'No.'

'You do not know where he is now?'

'No.'

'Is there a possibility of his returning and taking you away if he gets to know that you have inherited some money from your father?'

A few minutes' silence. Then—

'Yes.'

'You do not wish to be with him?'

'No.'

I noticed Tarashankar-babu smiling enigmatically.

Byomkesh changed his track.

'Where is your husband from?'

'Jessore.'

'Is his family still there?'

'No.'

'What about your father-in-law and mother-in-law?'

'Dead.'

'Where did your wedding take place?'

'Nabadwip.'

'Why don't you live with your cousins in Nabadwip? They are your father's brothers' children, after all.'

No answer.

'Don't you trust them?'

'No.'

'You consider Tarashankar-babu your greatest ally?'

'Yes.'

Byomkesh stared at the wall with a frown for some time, then resumed in a different direction—

'Barada-babu had proposed performing the last rites for your father in Gaya. Why didn't you agree?'

Unresponsive.

'You do not believe in all this?'

Still there was no answer.

'Never mind. Now tell me, did you hear anything the night your father died?'

'No.'

'Were the diamonds and precious stones kept in his bedroom?'

'Yes.'

'Where in the bedroom?'

'I don't know.'

'You cannot even hazard a guess?'

'No.'

'Did he have any enemies?'

'I don't know.'

'Didn't your father ever discuss his business with you?'

'No.'

'Your sleeping arrangements were on the ground floor. Which room did you sleep in?'

'In the room beneath my father's.'

'Your sleep was not disturbed on the night he was murdered?'

'No.'

'Very well, you may leave now,' Byomkesh told her with a sigh.

Thereafter our business at Tarashankar-babu's house ended. It was time to go. As we were about to leave, Tarashankar-babu told Byomkesh expansively, 'I am actually quite pleased to see you verify my claims. You are a man with insights; perhaps you will succeed in solving the mystery of Baikuntha's death. Come to me if you ever need help. And please remember that word must not spread about the money deposited with me. If it does, I shall be forced to lie.'

Emerging on the road, we turned back towards the fort. Daylight was about to fade like a woman lowering her eyes; the western sky glittered like a mirror streaked with vermilion. The crescent moon shone in the middle—like the reflected smile of a beautiful woman engaged in her toilette!

But Byomkesh did not have eyes for this scene; he walked on with his head sunk into his shoulders. After we had walked in silence for a few minutes, I asked him furtively, 'What did you think of Tarashankar-babu, Byomkesh?'

Raising his eyes to the sky, Byomkesh chuckled suddenly. 'He is a very wise man,' he replied.

4

As you entered the fort, Kailash-babu's house was situated at the end of the road on the left leading to the Ganga. It was a rather desolate spot. A small two-storied building stood amidst a low-walled garden, with a few casuarinas and deodar trees lining the perimeter. The location of the house suggested that Baikuntha-babu's murderer could not have been particularly afraid of being apprehended.

Barada-babu led us directly to Kailash-babu's bedroom on the first floor. The room was completely devoid of embellishments; only an iron bedstead was resplendent in the middle, upon which sat Kailash-babu, leaning against a pillow.

A servant fetched a few chairs, lit the lamp, and left. The kerosene lanterns suspended from the ceiling partly dispelled the grey exhaustion hanging heavily in the near-dark room. Munger did not boast of electric lights those days.

Kailash-babu's appearance left no room for doubt about his illness. He was quite fair of skin, but a waxen translucent paleness brought on by the disease seemed to have turned his complexion lifeless. A stubble made his face look even more emaciated than it was. His eyes were restive and accusing, while his voice had acquired a disgruntled sharpness from years of suffering.

We took our seats after introducing ourselves; Byomkesh went up to the window. There was just that one window in the room, facing west; the garden was visible below. The Ganges was visible in the distance through gaps in the row of deodar trees. There were no more houses here, the sandbanks of the river beginning on the other side of the wall.

Peering out, Byomkesh said, 'The window is about fifteen feet from the ground. Incredible!' Casting curious glances around the room, he took a seat too.

We discussed the supernatural events with Kailash-babu for some time; but no fresh light was cast on the matter. But we found him to be extraordinarily stubborn. He did not disbelieve the ghostly sighting; his words even revealed that he was noticeably terrified. But in no circumstances would he abandon the haunted house. Taking the condition of his heart into account, his doctor had advised him to shift his residence. His apprehensive companions had been coaxing him too, but like a sick child, he had clung obstinately to this house. He refused to budge.

Suddenly Kailash-babu said something that startled us. 'Everyone has told me to give this house up,' he said in his customary irascible tone. 'But my friends, how will it help if I do—for this will happen wherever I go. No one else knows the reason for all these supernatural goings-on, I alone know. You people are under the impression that some Baikuntha-babu's spirit is frequenting this place. That's not true at all—the real story is quite different.'

'What do you mean?' we asked curiously.

'Baikuntha my foot—this is the doing of a ghoul. The exploits of my worthy son.'

'What!'

Kailash-babu's waxen neck flushed faintly; sitting up straight, he said in agitation, 'Yes, the good-for-nothing boy has gone to the dogs. A gentleman's son, the only heir of a zamindar—and yet he wants to side with the devil! Have you ever heard of such a thing? Because I have disowned the scoundrel, he is up in arms against me. On top of which he has got himself a godless guru. I've been told they drink out of human skulls at the crematorium. They laid siege to my door one day; I had the doorman whip them and throw them out. So they have conspired to let loose a ghoul on me.'

'But . . .'

'The evil son that he is—can you not surmise his intentions? I have a bad heart; if I were to have a heart attack at the sight of a ghoul—that's all he wants! My dearest son will enjoy his inheritance with his ungodly guru without anything coming in the way!' Kailash-babu laughed bitterly; then, suddenly glancing at the window, he exclaimed in terror, 'There . . . there . . .'

We had been listening to him with our backs towards the window—we turned at lightning speed. It would not be surprising for the blood to run cold at the sight that confronted us. Darkness had fallen outside; in the dim light of the kerosene lamp we saw a grotesque face in the black frame of the window. All skin and bones, it was yellowish-white; a few yellow teeth visible through parted lips; the demonic look from a pair of ferocious, hungry eyes sunk in sockets with dark circles under them seemed desirous of devouring everything within the room.

For a moment we were paralysed. Then Byomkesh leapt to the window with a couple of strides. But the terrifying face had disappeared by then.

I raced up next to Byomkesh. Looking into the darkness, we thought we could discern a lean and very tall figure disappearing in the dense shade of the deodar trees.

Lighting a match, Byomkesh held it outside the window. Leaning out, I saw there was no ladder or any other means of climbing up the wall. In fact, there wasn't even a parapet on the wall that a person could stand on.

Byomkesh's match went out. He returned to his chair slowly.

Barada-babu had remained seated. 'Did you see it?' he said, turning to Byomkesh.

'I did.'

Barada-babu smiled dignifiedly, his eyes shining with victorious pride. 'What did it seem like?' he asked.

Kailash-babu answered. Now slumped on the bed, supported by his pillow, he exclaimed hopelessly, 'What could it have seemed like! It's a ghoul. It won't go without taking me. My time is near, Byomkesh-babu. Have you ever heard of anyone escaping a ghoul?' His terrified expression did suggest that his time was nigh, for his weakened heart would be unable to withstand such an assault on his nerves.

'Fear is our greatest enemy—not ghosts or ghouls,' said Byomkesh soothingly. 'My suggestion is, why not give up this house?'

'I agree,' added Barada-babu. 'I am convinced this house is under a bad star—it's not a matter of ghouls or anything. Ever since Baikuntha-babu's unnatural death . . .'

'Ghoul or Baikuntha-babu, the long and the short of it is that the state of Kailash-babu's health is such that shocks are not good for him. Therefore the correct course of action is to move from this house.'

'I shall not go.' An unyielding obduracy appeared on Kailash-babu's face. 'Why should I? Have I done anything wrong to flee like a criminal? If my own son wants me to die, very well, I shall die. I do not wish to continue living as the father of an evil son who is not afraid to kill his father.'

Arguing in the face of rage and obstinacy is wasted. It was late. We rose to leave; after assurances of returning the next morning, we went downstairs.

There was no conversation on the way back. Barada-babu attempted to speak once or twice, but Byomkesh paid no attention. Barada-babu walked back with us all the way to our house.

Shashanka-babu had returned meanwhile. 'Well, what happened?' he asked as soon as we entered.

Lying back in an easy chair, Byomkesh replied, 'The ghost made an appearance.' Sighing, he added, as though talking to himself, 'But Barada-babu's ghost and Kailash-babu's ghoul have joined hands to make the whole thing exceedingly complicated.'

The following day was Sunday. As soon as he had awakened in the morning, Byomkesh told Shashanka-babu, 'Let us pay a visit to Kailash-babu.'

'Do you want to see the ghost again?' asked Shashanka-babu. 'But what use is it visiting in daylight? The formless one can be seen only at night.'

'But we may see what does have form—what is material.'

'Very well, let us go.'

We arrived at our destination even before seven o' clock. Kailash-babu's house was not completely awake yet.

A drowsy servant was sweeping the veranda downstairs; the door to the householder's bedroom upstairs was still shut. 'No harm done,' said Byomkesh. 'Let us explore the garden meanwhile.'

The grass was moist with dew. The puckered surface of the deodar leaves glittered in the golden sunlight. The autumn morning was exquisitely spotless. We roamed all over the garden.

The garden was not less than an acre and a half in area, but there were no flowerbeds. A few balsam and oleander bushes were scattered, flowering in neglect. There was no gardener—possibly Baikuntha-babu had not employed one either. When the weeds grew too thick they were probably removed by the servants themselves.

We discovered evidence of this at the western extremity of the garden. A heap of refuse lay by the wall. Ash from the oven, kindling, scraps of paper, garbage . . . all of it was piled here. Compressed by the sun and the rain, there was a mound of refuse from many years.

Climbing upon the heap, Byomkesh looked around enquiringly. Toeing the earth and ash aside, he peered within. Finding an old tin, he examined it thoroughly before throwing it away. 'And what might you be looking for in the garbage?' asked Shashanka-babu, observing his actions.

Without lifting his eyes from the heap of ash, Byomkesh quoted Tagore, 'As our ancient poet has said, wherever you see ash, look beneath the surface, for you may find . . . what's that?'

A cracked, discarded lantern chimney lay there; picking it up, Byomkesh examined the shell. Then, gingerly inserting his fingers, he extracted a tattered piece of paper. It had probably been driven inside the chimney by the wind; and then made a long-standing home of it. Throwing the chimney away, Byomkesh looked closely at the paper. I went up to him in eagerness.

It was a portion of a printed handbill; it seemed to have indistinct images of animals. The elements had discoloured the paper; even the ink had faded so much that discerning the writing seemed impossible.

'What are you looking at?' asked Shashanka-babu. 'What have you got there?'

'Nothing.' Turning the piece of paper over, Byomkesh raised it closer to his eyes. 'There's something written by hand here. See if you can read it,' he told me, handing it over to me.

I examined it thoroughly. It was difficult to decipher at first. There was nothing left of the ink, only a few words could be guessed at from the scratches left by the nib—

Trouble . . . needmon

Or else . . . father . . . desperate

. . . your . . . badd . . .

I conveyed my reading to Byomkesh. 'Yes, that is what I thought too. Let me keep this.' Folding the piece of paper, he put it in his pocket.

'The writer was probably not very well educated,' I said. 'He wrote "badd".'

'The word may not be "bad"', responded Byomkesh.

'Let's go,' said Shashanka-babu a trifle impatiently. 'What's the use of rummaging in the ash heap. Kailash-babu must be awake by now.'

'Yes, I see his ghostly window is open,' said Byomkesh. 'Let us go.'

5

Approaching the house, we saw Kailash-babu at the window. A withered, pale face—if this had been night and not morning, no one who saw him suddenly at the window would have doubted that he was a ghost.

He invited us upstairs. Byomkesh ran his sharp eyes swiftly over the ground beneath the window. A thick carpet of green grass rolled all the way to the house; it betrayed no telltale signs.

Entering Kailash-babu's room, we saw that tea had been laid out. Although we had already had a round of tea, we had no objection to another.

The tea was accompanied by conversation. The continuous deterioration of the local weather, the continuous improvement in medical treatment, the qualities of empirical medicine, black magic, exorcism—nothing was omitted. In the course of this conversation, Byomkesh asked, 'You sleep with the window shut, aren't you?'

'Yes,' answered Kailash-babu. 'Ever since its appearance, I have been forced to sleep with the window shut—although the doctor has forbidden it. He wants me to breathe as much fresh air as possible—but I am caught in a bind. What do you think I should do?'

'Has it helped to keep the window shut?'

'Not particularly. But at least there's no sighting. Since it appears at the dead of night to rattle the window, I simply cannot sleep alone in the room; one of my servants sleeps on the floor.'

Rising to his feet when we had finished our tea, Byomkesh said, 'I shall now examine the room carefully. Please don't take it amiss, Shashanka—I am not casting aspersions on your—that is to say, the police's—abilities; but *muninancha matibhrama*—even the sages lose their heads at times. I am conducting this examination just in case something escaped your attention.'

'Very well—go ahead,' responded Shashanka-babu scathingly. 'But if you can unearth a clue to Baikuntha-babu's murderer after all these days, I'll consider you a wizard.'

'By all means,' smiled Byomkesh. 'But never mind all that. Was there no furniture at all in this room on the day of Baikuntha-babu's death?'

'I've already told you there was nothing but the bed made on the floor, a jar of water and the paan-case. Oh yes, a copper ear-pick was found too.'

'Very well. Do carry on talking, Kailash-babu, I shall not disturb you. I will merely move about the room.'

Thereupon Byomkesh began to prowl around the room. Sometimes looking up at the ceiling, sometimes casting his eyes at the floor, he moved about in silence with a careworn expression. Pausing at the window, he inspected the wooden shutters and frame carefully; barring and locking the door, he tested it. Then he resumed his tour of the room.

Kailash-babu and Shashanka-babu observed his movements with great curiosity. I forced them into a conversation. No matter how oblivious to his surroundings Byomkesh might be, being followed by three pairs of inquisitive eyes would undoubtedly distract him, making him self-conscious. Therefore, I began a discussion on the first thing I could think of in order to divert their attention. But still, our eyes as well as our interest remained centred on Byomkesh throughout our incoherent exchanges on different subjects.

A quarter of an hour passed this way. Then I found myself distracted by a story Shashanka-babu was telling about the police, my eyes were no longer following Byomkesh; surprised by a sudden chuckle, I turned towards him. Byomkesh was standing very close to the southern wall, looking at it with a smile.

'Now what?' asked Shashanka-babu. 'What are you chuckling at?'

'Magic,' answered Byomkesh. 'Come and take a look. I'm sure you haven't seen this before.' He indicated the wall.

We rose eagerly. At first we could see nothing on the whitewashed wall. But then, under close observation, I spotted a clear fingerprint at a height of about five feet from the ground. As though someone had applied pressure with their finger on the lime covering the wall before it had set, leaving a mark.

'It's a thumbprint,' announced Shashanka-babu, inspecting the mark with knitted brows. 'What is its significance?'

'Significance? *Muninancha matibhrama*. You did not spot this sign left by the murderer.'

'Murderer!' Shashanka-babu's eyebrows shot up in surprise. 'How do you know this fingerprint belongs to the murderer? It is true we did not notice it earlier, but I fail to understand why that implies it is the murderer's. It may belong to the mason who whitewashed the room; or to anyone else.'

'That is not impossible. But the question is, why should the mason leave his fingerprint on the wall?'

'Why should the murderer, for that matter?'

Byomkesh threw a sharp glance at Shashanka-babu; then he said, 'That is true. So you do not consider it significant?'

'I want to say that there is no evidence of its being significant.'

Exhaling, Byomkesh said, 'Your logic is impeccable. In the absence of evidence, nothing can be accepted as significant. Do you have a penknife in your pocket? Or an ear-pick?'

'I have a penknife. But why?'

Shashanka-babu offered the penknife with a disgruntled expression. Displeased by Byomkesh's discovery, he was probably trying to dismiss it. Yet, his point of view did not seem entirely illogical. A fingerprint on the wall—no one knew when and by whom it had been left—what possible importance could it have in unravelling the murder mystery? And even if it did belong to the murderer, how would that help either? When we had no idea who the murderer was, I could not understand what use the fingerprint would be.

But Byomkesh began to work the penknife around the fingerprint on the wall. After loosening the coating carefully, as soon as he inserted the tip of the penknife below the surface and prised it outwards, a portion of the plaster, with the fingerprint on it, came loose. Wrapping it in his handkerchief carefully and putting it in his pocket, Byomkesh told Kailash-babu, 'I'm afraid I've disfigured your wall. Please have the cavity filled up.' Then, turning to Shashanka-babu, he said, 'Come, Shashanka, we are done here for now. It is nine already, we should not bother Kailash-babu any longer. By the way, Kailash-babu, do you hear from your family regularly?'

'Who's going to write to me?' retorted Kailash-babu. 'You are aware of the exploits of my only son; I have no other family to write to me.'

'How unfortunate,' said Byomkesh cheerfully. 'Well, we shall take your leave now; we shall be turning up from time to time to disturb you. And I would suggest not telling anyone about this.' Byomkesh pointed to the cavity in the wall.

Kailash-babu nodded his assent.

We went out on the road. The sun had become stronger now. We walked swiftly in the direction of our home.

'What is your real opinion about the fingerprint, Byomkesh?' Shashanka-babu asked suddenly.

'I have already given you my opinion; it is the murderer's fingerprint.'

'But this is obstinate insistence on your part,' responded Shashanka-babu testily. 'We do not have the slightest knowledge of the murderer's identity—and yet you claim it's the murderer's print. There has to be a valid reason, after all.'

'What kind of valid reason do you want to be presented with?'

Shashanka-babu could conceal his annoyance no longer. 'There's nothing I want to be presented with,' he exclaimed. 'I think you're being childish. It's not your fault, however; you probably think that the methods of investigation practised in Bengal can be applied here as well. That's where you're wrong. That kind of detective-work won't do here.'

'I did not come here to apply my detecting skills,' said Byomkesh. 'On the contrary, I am here to give them a rest. If you would prefer that I do not interfere in this matter I shall be relieved.'

'No, that is not what I am implying,' answered Shashanka-babu, controlling himself. 'What I intend to say is that the route you are taking will never get you anywhere—this isn't such a simple affair.'

'I can see as much.'

'If you imagine that a single fingerprint can help you solve a case that we have been unable to get to the bottom of even after six months, it must be concluded that you have failed to realize the importance of this affair. A fingerprint or a couple of handwritten words on a scrap of paper found in a heap of rubbish can make for mystery novels, but not for police investigations. Which is why I'm advising you to abandon all this fingerprint business and . . .'

'Stop!'

A phaeton was passing; spotting us, its occupant instructed the driver to stop; poking his head out, he asked, 'Any progress, Byomkesh-babu?'

Tarashankar-babu was on his way back after a dip in the Ganga; he had earth smeared on his forehead, a shawl with the names of the gods embroidered on it around his shoulder, and a sarcastic smile on his face.

'With what?' Byomkesh asked innocently.

'What do you suppose? Baikuntha's murder, obviously. Found anything?'

'Why are you asking me about this?' said Byomkesh. 'I am not supposed to find anything. You had better ask Shashanka.'

Arching his left eyebrow slightly, Tarashankar-babu said, 'But did I not hear that you have been given fresh responsibility for investigating this case? Be that as it may, what news, Shashanka-babu? Any new discoveries?'

'Even if there are, I do not have the authority to publicly reveal facts known only to the police,' answered Shashanka-babu insipidly. 'And you have been misinformed—Byomkesh is my friend; he is on holiday in Munger and has nothing to do with the investigation.'

Affection between a policeman and a lawyer is exceedingly rare. I observed there was no love lost between Tarashankar-babu and Shashanka-babu. Pouring honey into his voice, Tarashankar-babu said, 'I see, so you have found nothing. I had already concluded that the police would not succeed in achieving anything more . . . Go!'

Tarashankar-babu's phaeton left.

What Shashanka-babu said sotto voce, looking angrily in the direction of the retreating phaeton, was not an endearment. We were all annoyed. No further conversation ensued on the way, and we reached home in silence.

6

Byomkesh passed the afternoon in indolence. He gave a single careless glance at the scrap of paper and the fingerprint before putting them away again. I was unable to understand the working of his mind; but it appeared that the interest he had felt all this while in this murder had waned.

Barada-babu arrived late in the afternoon. 'We have a Bengali club here,' he said, 'shall we pay them a visit?'

'Certainly.'

We had been in town for two days already, but had not yet seen any of the sights; so Barada-babu took us to the Kashtaharini Ghat, Peer Shanfa's tomb, and several other landmarks. Then, after sunset, he shepherded us to the club.

It was situated outside the fort. On the way, we saw an enormous tent pitched in the middle of a field; a crowd had gathered around it—bright lights and western music emanated from it.

'What's that?' I asked.

'The circus is in town.'

'Do you get circuses here?' asked Byomkesh.

'Of course we do,' answered Barada-babu. 'They charge a pretty penny too. There was a troupe last year as well—no, not last year, but the year before.'

'How long have they been here?'

'They started their shows yesterday.'

In this context, Barada-babu complained of the lack of entertainment avenues in town. The few Bengalis there were in town were all engaged in endless factionalism; hence, although there was an amateur theatre group, there weren't many performances. The carnivals that visited now and then were the only hope. Bengalis try to compensate for the lack of pomp and diversity in their real lives by playing kings and generals in plays. Therefore, wherever there were at least two Bengalis, there was bound to be an amateur theatre group, and wherever there was a theatre group, factionalism was inevitable. It was hardly surprising, then, that entertainment was dependent on imported acts.

We arrived at the club, the complaints ringing in our ears.

The entrance to the club was narrow but accessible. Several rooms were arranged around an open space. Entering, we discovered a sheet spread out on the floor of one of the rooms, with a few of the members seated on it, playing bridge; at the end of each rubber their voices rose in criticism, but everyone turned silent and serious as soon as the next rubber commenced. In no circumstances could their attention be drawn to anything beyond the game; no one noticed the arrival of two strangers. Two members were in a state of trance in one corner over their chessboard; not even a bevy of dancing nymphs would be able to break their severe penance till the game was over.

The excited voices of some other members could be heard in the next room—Barada-babu led us in there. Several young men were sitting around a table—among them Shailen-babu, whom we had met already. Surrounding him like a phalanx, the rest of them had overwhelmed him with pointed, sceptical arrows about ghosts and spirits.

At the sight of Barada-babu, a faint hope of rescue surfaced in Shailen-babu's eyes; extending his hand, he said, 'Welcome, Barada-babu, these people here have . . . Ah, you're here too, Byomkesh-babu. Do come in.'

The debate was stopped by the arrival of two newcomers. When we had sat down after being introduced by Barada-babu, he asked, 'What's everyone so agitated about? What's the matter?'

'They refuse to believe that I saw the ghost,' answered Shailen-babu. 'They claim it was a figment of my imagination.'

'What we want to say is that a spate of Barada's old wives' tales have led him to the point where he sees ghosts everywhere,' declared a gentleman named Prithwish-babu. 'He's probably mistaken a bat or some such creature for a ghost.'

'I admit to not having seen anything clearly,' said Sailen-babu. 'But I can swear it wasn't a bat. And if you accuse me of having lost my eyesight from Barada-babu's stories . . .'

'These two gentlemen arrived yesterday,' Barada-babu said grimly, indicating us. 'Do you think I have converted them too with my stories?'

'No, we don't,' answered one of the combatants. 'But if you have enough time . . .'

'They saw the ghost last night,' announced Barada-babu.

Everyone fell silent. Then Prithwish-babu asked Byomkesh, 'You really did?'

'Yes,' admitted Byomkesh.

'What did you see?'

'A face.'

The enemy side exchanged glances. Byomkesh described the circumstances in which the face had appeared. Silence ensued again. The joy of victory showed on Barada-babu's and Shailen-babu's countenances.

Amulya-babu had sat by quietly all this while, without joining the argument. His face reflected a conflict between unwilling acceptance and suppressed scepticism. His mind was in the state that comes from being compelled to believe that which we do not want to believe—he would be relieved if he could somehow strike at the root cause of this unwelcome acceptance. Now he spoke, purging his voice of combative contempt as much as he could, 'That may be so. Since many people say they have seen the ghost, let us accept it as a true story. But why? Assuming that Baikuntha the jeweller has indeed become a ghost, how does it benefit him to haunt Kailash-babu? Can someone explain this to me?'

'You cannot always get to the bottom of the intentions of ghosts and spirits,' responded Barada-babu. 'But I believe that Baikuntha-babu wishes to say something.'

'If he wants to, why doesn't he?' snapped Amulya-babu.

'He isn't getting the opportunity. His appearance frightens us so much that he is forced to leave. Besides, the power to assume the form of a spirit does not always imply having the power to speak too. Ectoplasm, which is the substance of the form that . . .'

'Never mind the pedantry, Barada. We know you have memorized all those books on spiritualism. But if your Baikuntha-babu lacks the power of speech, why is he needlessly pestering an innocent man?'

'Even if he cannot actually speak, there are ways to make him communicate.'

'What ways?'

'The planchette table.'

'That three-legged table business? That's nothing but a hoax.'

'How do you know? Have you ever tried it?'

Amulya-babu was forced into silence. Turning to us, Barada-babu said, 'I am convinced Baikuntha-babu has something to say; maybe he wishes to disclose the identity of the murderer. We should help him. He might be able to communicate if we summon him using the planchette table. Would you like to try?'

Never having seen a spirit being summoned, I was eager. 'Why not?' I answered. 'Shall we try right away?'

'No harm,' responded Barada-babu. 'Let us try right here—do you agree? If we can summon a spirit, your scepticism will be dispelled.'

Everyone concurred with enthusiasm.

A small table was fetched at once. Barada-babu said that too many cooks would spoil the broth, so five people were selected. Barada-babu, Byomkesh, Shailen-babu, Amulya-babu and I remained in the room. The rest shifted to the adjoining chamber.

Dimming the lights, we drew our chairs up to the table. Barada-babu explained the method to us briefly. Placing our hands on the table and touching one another's fingers lightly, we shut our eyes and began to think of Baikuntha-babu. Near-darkness and complete silence prevailed.

Five minutes passed this way. There was no sign of the

ghost. Other thoughts strayed into my mind; I forced myself to concentrate on Baikuntha-babu alone. Just as I was getting impatient at this tug of war, the table seemed to move slightly. My skin prickled suddenly. I sat motionless, the nerves in my finger-ends unusually sensitive.

The table moved again, as though it were turning slowly under my fingers.

Barada-babu's baritone was heard. 'Are you here, Baikuntha-babu? Knock once if you are.'

There was no response at first. Then one of the feet of the table rose in the air slowly before falling back on the ground with a sound.

'He is here,' declared Barada-babu solemnly but softly.

My nerves tingled even more; my ears began to buzz. But I was surprised when I opened my eyes. I do not know what I was expecting, but all I saw was all five of us sitting as before in half-darkness. It was impossible to perceive the significant change that had taken place—that a spirit had appeared somewhere close to us from the afterlife.

'May I ask the questions?' Barada-babu said softly.

We nodded. He proceeded to question the spirit in measured tones.

'What do you want?'

There was no answer. The table was immobile.

'Why do you keep appearing?'

The table seemed to move a little. But even after a long wait, there was no clear response.

'Do you have something to say?'

This time the leg of the table clearly rose in the air. It knocked several times on the floor—but no meaning was evident.

'Knock once for yes, knock twice for no,' instructed Barada-babu.

A single knock was heard.

I realized that the process of exchanging thoughts with the afterlife was not particularly simple. It was still possible to indicate a 'yes' or a 'no'; but for a spirit to communicate in detail was considerably difficult. Still, human intelligence had managed to overcome this obstacle to an extent—the practice of conveying letters through numbers was prevalent. This was the practice that Barada-babu adopted; addressing the spirit, he said, 'Spell out what you want to say letter by letter, using the number of knocks to indicate each letter.'

The telegraphic communication began. The leg of the table knocked, then fell silent; it knocked again, and fell silent again. The statement that emerged with much effort after a long time was this:

Vacate . . . the . . . house . . . or . . . else . . . harm . . .

After the last knock of the table had faded away, we sat stupefied with fear for some time. Then, clearing his throat, Barada-babu said, 'We will try to ensure that your house is vacated. Is there anything else that you would like to tell us?'

The table was immobile.

A thought occurred to me suddenly; secretly I whispered to Barada-babu, 'Ask him who the murderer is.'

Barada-babu asked the question. There was no answer for some time; then the leg rose.

Ta . . . ra . . . ta . . . ra . . . ta . . . ra . . .

Suddenly the table shook violently several times and then came to a standstill. 'We do not understand,' Barada-babu said, his voice shaking. 'Tara . . . and then? Is that someone's name?'

The table was immobile.

'Are you still here?' Barada-babu asked again.

There was no answer, the table had become an inanimate object.

'He's gone,' sighed Barada-babu.

Byomkesh reached out to turn up the light; then, casting a sharp glance at everyone's hands, he said, somewhat brusquely, 'Excuse me, but no one should remove their hands from the table. I would like to examine your hands.'

'You wish to check whether any of us has glue on our hands?' asked Barada-babu with a faint smile. 'Very well, go ahead.'

I was extremely embarrassed by Byomkesh's behaviour. To openly suggest all these gentlemen of fraud was simply not done. Doubtless he was deeply suspicious—but still, he had no right to conduct such a harsh investigation to assess the truth. Everyone must have been disappointed; but Byomkesh unabashedly examined our hands. He did not spare me either.

But no one's hands yielded anything of significance.

Placing his cheek in his palm, and resting his elbows on the table, Byomkesh stared blankly at the light.

'So you found nothing?' asked Barada-babu, throwing a challenge.

'Extraordinary,' answered Byomkesh. 'You cannot even imagine such a thing.'

'There are more things . . .' pronounced Barada-babu happily in English, quoting Shakespeare.

Amulya-babu's doubts had evaporated completely, he asked incoherently, 'But . . . did any of you make sense of tara . . .?'

Everyone exchanged glances. The answer flashed in my mind suddenly—Tarashankar. I was about to say the name out loud when Byomkesh clamped a hand over my mouth, saying, 'It's best not to discuss this.'

'Yes, let whatever we have learnt remain with us,' remarked Barada-babu. Everyone agreed, with perturbed expressions.

'This was an extraordinary experience—I still cannot believe it,' said Byomkesh. 'And yet I have no choice but to believe it. Thank you for this, Barada-babu.' He rose to his feet.

Shailen-babu and Amulya-babu accompanied us on the way back home, along with Barada-babu. Their homes were inside the fort.

When we were close to our home, Shailen-babu said, 'I live alone, I have my doubts whether I'll sleep tonight.'

'What have you got to be afraid of?' observed Barada-babu. 'It's Kailash-babu who should be afraid. How do you think we can persuade him to shift?'

'We simply have to convince him to abandon the house,' said Byomkesh. 'All of you are trying already, so shall I. Kailash-babu is a stubborn man, but we have to do this for his sake. Meanwhile we are home now, please do not trouble yourself any more. Good night.'

Bidding us good night, they went on their way. We could hear Amulya-babu saying, 'You'd better spend the night at my house, Shailen-babu. You stay alone, there is no one else at my house either at present . . .'

Evidently the planchette session had cast a shadow of terror on everyone.

7

Shashanka-babu had probably lost faith in Byomkesh; so he did not bring up the subject of the murder after our return from Kailash-babu's house that day. Besides, his workload had suddenly increased, and with the Puja vacation around the corner, he did not have the opportunity either.

Thereafter, we spent the next two or three days rambling around the town and its outskirts. It was an ancient place, with many legends and historical tales having been gathered from the age of Jarasandha to the era of Robert Clive. The town was irresistible to those with a penchant for history.

As we wandered about, Byomkesh seemed to have forgotten all about the murder. His only activity in this connection was to visit Kailash-babu's house every evening and entice him in different ways into moving out of the house. His skilfully-constructed arguments seemed to be bearing fruit, with Kailash-babu beginning to show signs of reluctant agreement.

Eventually, he assented after a week or thereabouts. A suitable house had been located outside the fort—it was decided that he would shift to this building the following Sunday.

On Sunday morning, Byomkesh said over our morning tea, 'Shashanka, we should weigh anchor now. We have been here for quite some time.'

'Already!' exclaimed Shashanka-babu. 'Why don't you stay a little longer? You don't have anything urgent to attend to in Calcutta, do you?' What he said was consonant with courtesy, but his voice lacked fervour.

'Perhaps not,' answered Byomkesh. 'But still, one has to keep the shop open in anticipation of business.'

'That is true. When are you thinking of going?'

'Today. We have spent a singularly agreeable holiday—I shall remember this for a long time.'

'Today? Well . . . suit yourself . . .' Shashanka-babu looked out the window for a few minutes, and then said somewhat glumly, 'But this whole business hasn't been cleared. I do not deny that it is a complex affair, but considering your reputation, I had expected you to solve this case.'

'What are you referring to?'

'Baikuntha-babu's murder. Have you forgotten?'

'Oh—no, I have not. But there's nothing more to learn there.'

'Nothing to learn! What do you mean? Have you learnt all there is?'

'Well, you could certainly say that.'

'What! I don't understand,' declared Shashanka-babu, turning in his chair to face Byomkesh.

'Why, I've known for several days all there is to know about Baikuntha-babu's murder,' announced Byomkesh, his voice tinged with surprise. 'Do we need to rack our brains over it now?'

Shashanka-babu stared at him dumbfounded. 'But . . . you've known for several days . . . what are you saying? Have you come to know who killed Baikuntha-babu?'

'But I came to know that last Sunday.'

'Then . . . why didn't you tell me all this while?'

'Frankly, your behaviour suggested that the police do not wish for my assistance,' Byomkesh answered with a faint smile. 'The methods we apply in Bengal appear laughable here, your contempt for fingerprints and scraps of paper is boundless. That is why I did not volunteer to speak up. Just imagine how terrible it would be for me if the entire police community were to mock at my explanation, dismissing it as the stuff of a sensational thriller.'

'But . . . you could have told me personally,' Shashanka-babu gulped. 'I'm your friend, after all! Never mind all that, now tell me what you have learnt.' He pulled his chair close to Byomkesh's.

Byomkesh was silent.

'Who is the murderer? Do we know him?'

Byomkesh smiled.

Putting his hand on Byomkesh's knee, Shashanka-babu practically pleaded, 'Tell me Byomkesh, who did it?'

'The ghost.'

Flabbergasted, Shashanka-babu stared blankly for a few moments. Then he said, 'Are you joking? The ghost murdered him?'

'Meaning . . . yes, just that.'

'Don't beat about the bush, Byomkesh,' said Shashanka-babu impatiently. 'If you really believe that the ghost committed the murder . . . then . . .' He gestured hopelessly with his hand.

Byomkesh chuckled. After a turn around the veranda, he said, 'If I have to explain everything to you clearly, I cannot leave today—I'll have to stay the night. You will not understand until I have turned the accused in to the police. Kailash-babu is shifting house today; therefore I am hopeful of nabbing the murderer tonight.' He paused, then continued. 'It's just that one feels unhappy for Baikuntha-babu's daughter. Never mind all that, now let me explain what we must do.'

It was autumn, the days were getting shorter. It was dark by six o' clock, and by nine o' clock the inhabitants of the fort took to their beds and fell asleep. We had noticed as much over the past few days.

The three of us left home shortly before nine o' clock

that night. Byomkesh took a torch, while Shashanka-babu slipped a pair of handcuffs into his pocket.

The road was empty of people; clouds had gathered in the sky, obliterating the half-moon. The dim kerosene lamps burning atop lampposts situated at long intervals along the road merely succeeded in making the impenetrable darkness of the night murkier. We did not meet a soul on the way.

When we reached Kailash-babu's abandoned house, the clock at the government treasury was ringing nine. Glancing up and down the road, Shashanka-babu whistled softly; a man emerged from the darkness—we could not see him, we only made out his presence from indistinct footsteps. Byomkesh said something to him quietly, whereupon he vanished again.

We entered the house warily. It was empty, all the doors and windows were open—not a light was to be seen anywhere. The house was as inert as a lifeless corpse.

We tiptoed upstairs. Byomkesh paused for a moment at the door to Kailash-babu's room; entering, he switched the torch on and swept its beam over the room. The room was empty—the bed and everything else had been shifted along with Kailash-babu. A cool breeze from the Ganga wafted into the bare room through the open window.

Shutting the door, Byomkesh switched the torch off. Then, squatting on the floor, he said softly, 'Sit down. There's no telling how long we have to wait; we may have to be here till three in the morning. Ajit, as soon as I switch the torch on, you will go to the window and guard it; and Shashanka, you will perform the duty of the policeman—that is to say, hold the ghost with all your might.'

Then we began our vigil in the darkness. We sat in silence, motionless; the slightest movement or sound evoked annoyance from Byomkesh. Lighting a cigarette to cremate time was out of the question too; the smell would scare the prey away.

The treasury clock announced the hour—it was now past eleven o' clock. There was no knowing when he would turn up. Meanwhile my eyelids were growing heavy.

Telling myself that the evening had just begun, I had barely opened my mouth in surrender to an unconquerable urge to yawn when Byomkesh clamped his fingers on my knee. The yawn ended abruptly halfway.

There was a sound near the window. I could see nothing; only a low, indistinct sound penetrated my senses. It was not repeated. I held my breath in an attempt to listen, but I could hear nothing—only a hammering in my heart like a drum kept growing stronger.

Suddenly I was startled by the rustle of someone dragging his feet across the floor very close to us. A person had entered the room, and was no more than a couple of feet away—but I could not see him at all. Was he aware of our presence in the room? Who was he? What would he do now? A chill ran down my spine.

Just like the rays of the morning sun entering the room through a crack in the barred door, a sliver of light came to life in the middle of the room, falling on the wall before us. It was an exceedingly thin beam, but it appeared to brighten the room. We saw a tall, dark figure standing with his back to us, seeking something on the wall with the light from a torch in his hand.

Advancing towards the wall, the dark figure examined the layer of lime on it with great concentration. An inarticulate sound emerged from his throat, as though he had found what he was seeking.

Byomkesh switched on his torch. I was momentarily blinded by the dazzle. Then I raced to the window to take up a position before it.

The stranger had turned in a flash, shielding his eyes with his hand. I could not see his face. Then several events took place almost simultaneously. The intruder sprang at me like a tiger, Shashanka-babu leapt on him, and all three of us went down on the floor in a huddle.

But the struggle and thrashing about did not stop. Shashanka-babu tried to pin the intruder to the ground like a wrestler; he bit Shashanka-babu sharply on the shoulder and jumped to his feet. But Shashanka-babu wasn't going to give up easily; he clung to the intruder's feet. The stranger could not shake him off; he advanced towards the window, dragging Shashanka-babu behind him. Now I caught a glimpse of his contorted, grotesquely painted face in the light of torch. A ghost indeed.

Byomkesh said calmly, 'You will only suffer if you try to escape through the window, Shailen-babu. Your stilts are no longer there; they have been removed by constable Bhanupratap Singh and his associates, who are waiting for you.' Raising his voice, he continued, 'Please come upstairs, Constable Singh.'

The grotesque face turned towards me. Shailen-babu! Our harmless Shailen-babu . . . in this form! I was numb with astonishment.

For a few moments, the demonic, hungry eyes on Shailen-babu's contorted face, turned towards Byomkesh, seemed about to burst. Baring his teeth like a feral beast, he attempted to say something; but only something akin to a groan emerged. Suddenly he slumped to the ground.

When Shashanka-babu had risen to his feet after letting go of Shailen-babu's legs, Byomkesh said, 'Shashanka, you may know Shailen-babu, but you are probably not aware of his actual identity. I see your shoulder is bleeding; it isn't serious, a spot of tincture iodine will be sufficient. Besides, since you have accepted a position with the police, you will certainly have to accept the side effects of the job. Never mind all that, let me reveal Shailen-babu's real identity. He is a well-known gymnast at the circus—and Baikuntha-babu's missing son-in-law. If he has in fact only bitten you on your shoulder, you could consider it as the proverbial joke on the part of the son-in-law.

But Shashanka-babu was unable to consider it a joke; with a muted roar he clamped his handcuffs on the son-in-law's wrists. At that very moment, constable Bhanupratap

Singh arrived in the room, complete with his giant whiskers and curling moustache, and saluted.

8

Glancing at his watch, Byomkesh said, 'Only seventeen minutes to go. Therefore I shall present my explanation swiftly before departing for the station.'

It is needless to describe the sensation caused in the town by the arrest of Baikuntha-babu's murderer. Somehow people had come to know that it was Byomkesh who had made the impossible come true. Despite trying his best to maintain an air of affection as well as satisfaction, Shashanka-babu had failed miserably at the task. Therefore we had decided to return to Calcutta without any further unnecessary delay.

Kailash-babu had returned to his former residence. We were gathered in his bedroom before our departure. Shashanka-babu, Barada-babu and Amulya-babu were present; half-sitting, half-lying on his bed, Kailash-babu was striving to summon an unfamiliarly pleasant expression to his countenance. His remorse for falsely suspecting his son was evident.

'Now I realize that it was neither a ghost nor a ghoul but Shailen-babu,' he exclaimed suddenly. 'Oh, how devious the man is! Do you remember how he had sat here in this room and cried "there . . . there!"? All lies. He had seen nothing—he was merely trying to deceive us. So that we could not imagine that he himself was the ghost. Now, Byomkesh-babu, pray explain how you solved the mystery.'

Everyone looked at Byomkesh eagerly.

With a smile, Byomkesh began. 'Do not take it amiss, Barada-babu, but I was always a disbeliever when it came to ghosts and spirits. I am not getting into the question of their existence; but I suspected from the beginning that the creature appearing in Kailash-babu's presence was not a spirit but a flesh and blood human being. I am a mere materialist, I deal in material objects; therefore, I always keep extra-sensory matters out of my calculations.

'Now let us assume that the ghost is in fact a human being. The question that naturally arises is: who is he and why would he behave thus? Why would a person frighten everyone who lives here by pretending to be a ghost? The only answer is that he wished to drive everyone away. Think about it, there cannot possibly be any other reasonable explanation.

'Very well. Now the question is—why does he wish to drive them away? Surely he has some motive in doing this. What is that motive?

'As all of you are aware, not a trace of Baikuntha-babu's valuable jewels was found after his death. The police suspect that he stashed them in a wooden box, which the murderer took after killing him. But I was unable to accept this contention without question. What little I have learnt of Miser Baikuntha's personality does not suggest that he was the kind of person to hoard his valuables in a simple wooden box. No one knew where he actually kept them. And yet, they were definitely in this very room. The question, then, is—where?

'But let us abandon this question for the moment. The only logical explanation for this nuisance of ghosts was that Baikuntha-babu's assailant knew where the valuables were hidden, but had not yet had the opportunity to take them away. Therefore he was trying to drive away the new inhabitants of this house, so that he could take away the riches without impediments.

'It is clear, then, that the ghost is actually Baikuntha-babu's murderer.

'When I interrogated Baikuntha-babu's daughter, two inconsistencies occurred to me from her responses. First, she had heard nothing that night. This seemed impossible. Despite occupying the room beneath this one, she heard nothing of the frantic struggle that took place when her father was strangled to death. The assailant had extracted information from the victim about the whereabouts of the jewels as he was choking him—in other words, they had had a conversation. Baikuntha-babu may have screamed too—yet his daughter heard nothing. Is this possible?

'Secondly, she is unwilling to perform the last rites for her departed father in Gaya to ensure salvation for his soul. The truth is that she knows that her father has not in fact become a spirit haunting his former home, which is why she was confident. Indeed, she was probably aware of the identity of this so-called spirit. There is no other explanation for a scarcely educated woman's refusing to perform her father's last rites.

'There is room for different kinds of speculation about Baikuntha-babu's daughter—we do not need to delve into each of them. But the primary one among them is that she knows who committed the murder, and that she is trying to protect the assailant. Who is closer to a woman than even her father? An answer is unnecessary. I had learnt the very first day that Baikuntha-babu's daughter is chaste of character. Therefore it could not have been anyone but her husband.

'I had gathered one more indication early on that Baikuntha-babu's son-in-law was the murderer. The ghost was fifteen feet tall, and able to peep through a first-floor window with ease. How could this be possible for an ordinary person? He had not employed a ladder either—it would have been impossible to disappear so quickly while carrying one. Well then? The answer—stilts. I am sure you know what they are. A pair of long sticks, with whose help dacoits would traverse thirty or forty miles to rob a distant house and return home, all in the space of a single night. At present, many circuses have performers who use stilts for their performance. No one can use stilts without regular practice. Therefore the assumption that the murderer might be a circus performer cannot be dismissed out of hand. Baikuntha-babu's prodigal son-in-law is part of a circus troupe; he must be an adept performer too—therefore the assumption is automatically strengthened.

'But everyone knows the son-in-law isn't here—he has been missing for eight years.

'Searching the garden the other day, I discovered this piece of paper in the refuse. A tattered old circus handbill, the picture of the lion on it not quite obliterated. A few handwritten words were visible on its back. It appeared as though someone had written a note on the back of the handbill because no other paper was available. The words were incoherent, but they seemed to yield a meaning—a penurious husband was seeking money from his wife. Ajit, the word you had interpreted as "bad" was actually "band"—a fragment of "husband".

'Evidently, a desperately bankrupt husband had written from a distant land to his wife. Needless to add, he had not received any financial assistance. It can scarcely be believed that Baikuntha-babu would offer monetary help to the scoundrel who had deserted his wife.

'All this had transpired some twelve months ago. There has not been a circus party in this town in the past two years; therefore it must be concluded that the husband had written this letter from a distant land and that he was with the circus at the time—using the back of a handbill in the absence of paper.

'A few months later, the husband arrived at Munger. I do not know how he had come into some money meanwhile; he proceeded to live here in the guise of someone seeking to restore his health. No one knew him in Munger—he was from Jessore and his wedding had taken place in

Nabadwip—which was why he had no fear of being found out as Baikuntha-babu's son-in-law.

'Baikuntha-babu had possibly never become aware of his son-in-law's arrival—he remained quite unperturbed. But the son-in-law made clandestine enquiries and formulated a plan; since the father-in-law would not part with his riches voluntarily, he resolved to extract his legacy by force.

'Then he went to his father-in-law's house that night on stilts, arriving directly in this father-in-law's bedroom through the window. The father-in-law was rather disturbed at this unexpected appearance, but the son-in-law was adamant. First he discovered the location of the jewels by strangling his father-in-law, then he killed him altogether. Baikuntha-babu's survival would have proved troublesome, which was why he had come prepared to murder him.

'But he did not have the opportunity to spirit away the treasure. His wife had woken up downstairs, and was now knocking on the door.

'The son-in-law fled quickly for the night with only a single gem in his possession. The rest remained where they were.

'Baikuntha-babu had hidden his jewels in a strange location—inside the walls of his room. Scraping off the surface of the wall and gouging a small hole in it, he would place a gem within it and refill the hole with lime. His paan-box contained enough lime for the purpose, making the task easy.

'Before extracting one of the jewels from the wall, the son-in-law quickly refilled the hole with lime. But in his haste, he could not do a smooth job of it, leaving his thumbprint behind.

'At first, I had also wondered where Baikuntha-babu had hidden his jewels. When I noticed the fingerprint the other day while examining the room, it all became clear to me in an instant. Jewels worth some two-and-a-half lakh rupees are concealed all over this room behind a layer of lime. They are hidden in a manner that will escape all but the most intense scrutiny. You will have to work hard to extricate these fifty-and-odd jewels, Shashanka. I do not have enough time, else I would have done it myself. Still, I have marked the spots with a pencil, so it should not prove difficult.

'So we are apprised of the fact that the son-in-law decamped with a single gem after murdering the father-in-law. And that he is engaged in attempts to seize the rest. But who is this son-in-law? He is certain to be an inhabitant of this town, and possibly familiar to us. We do have his fingerprint, but that alone cannot enable us to identify him amongst a town full of people. What is the way out, then?

'I got an opportunity at the planchette table the other evening. A ghost appeared at the table. I realized that one of us was shaking the table, and it had to be the murderer; the ghost's testimony was sufficient proof. I examined everyone's palms on a pretext. The fingerprint matched Shailen-babu's.

'Therefore there remained no further doubt that Shailen-babu was the murderer. Possibly none of you doubts it any more either. It had become rather simple for Shailen-babu to achieve his objective by becoming Barada-babu's disciple. The man appears innocent and honey-tongued on the surface, but he is as ferocious and cruel as a tiger within. There is no room for compassion in his heart.'

Byomkesh stopped. Everyone was silent. Eventually Amulya-babu said, exhaling loudly, 'Ah, I'm relieved. Apart from everything else, Byomkesh-babu, you have extricated us from Barada's ghosts. The way he was going on, I would have soon become a believer too; you have exorcized Barada's ghost, a million thanks for that.'

Everyone laughed. Barada-babu muttered something; Amulya-babu asked, 'What's that you're mumbling? It sounded like Sanskrit.'

'*Mouktikangnagajegaje*,' replied Barada-babu. 'Not finding the pearl on a single elephant's head does not mean it does not exist.'

'I have never searched the head of an elephant,' responded Amulya-babu, 'but all of us know perfectly well what lies in yours.'

'My seventeen minutes have passed,' said Byomkesh, rising to his feet. 'I shall take your leave now. I have said goodbye to Tarashankar-babu already—his is a generous soul. Convey my respectful greetings to him once more. Come along, Ajit.'

The Death of Amrito

1

The village was named Baghmari. It was situated just by the railway line, but to reach the village one had to walk about a mile from the station. Between the two lay a dense forest. The villagers did not usually enter the forest when going to and from the station—they slipped under the barbed wire protecting the railway line and walked along the tracks instead.

The station was named Santalgola. It was quite a large station, and a small town had sprung up around it. The area was rich in paddy. Both paddy and rice were exported from the region. There were a couple of rice mills too.

During the war, a company of American soldiers had camped for some time in the forest between Santalgola and Baghmari; they used to wander about bare-bodied, dressed only in trousers, and share a smoke with the farmers.

They returned home after the war, leaving behind several illegitimate children and some small arms.

The assignment on which Byomkesh and I were in Santalgola for some length of time was related to the abovementioned arms, details of which I shall disclose at the appropriate time. The story I am relating at present is set primarily in the village of Baghmari, and the individuals from whom I had heard the early parts of this tale were all young men from the village. In order to sacrifice verbosity, I am writing their testimonies in abridged form.

Of the handful of full-fledged houses in Bagmari village, Sadananda Sur's was the oldest. It comprised about three rooms, a paved courtyard in front, and another yard at the back with a wall running around it. The jungle began immediately behind the house.

Sadananda Sur was getting on in years, but since he had no family or wife or children, he lived all by himself in his ancestral home. He did have a solitary sister who was married to a railway employee, but they were townspeople to whom Sadananda-babu enjoyed no particular proximity. His relationship with other people in the village was not very close; while there was no antagonism with anyone, there was no intimacy either. On most days he awoke early and went to the station-town, returning to the village in the evening. Nobody knew what exactly he did for a living. Some said he was a broker dealing in paddy and rice; others said he ran a pawnshop. In sum, he was rather a secretive and thrifty person, which was about all that people knew about him.

One April morning, Sadananda left his home early; bringing a medium-sized trunk and a canvas bag out of the house, he locked the door. Then, holding one in each hand, he proceeded on his journey.

There was a clearing in front of the house, almost a field. As Sadananda was on his way towards the railway lines after walking across the field, he ran into Hiru, the village headman of advancing years. 'Where are we off to with all those boxes first thing in the morning?'

'I'm going away for a few days,' answered Sadananda.

'Ah,' responded Hiru. 'Pilgrimage?'

Sadananda merely smiled.

'Already thinking of atoning for your sins?' remarked Hiru. 'How old are you?'

'Forty-five.' Sadananda continued on his way.

'When will you be back?' Hiru called behind him.

'In a week or so.'

Sadananda left.

His sudden pilgrimage became a minor subject of discussion in the village. No one had suspected his soul of yearning for religious rituals. He had not spent a single night outside the village in the past ten years. Everyone assumed that Sadananda Sur, who usually went about his business without drawing attention to himself, was travelling on some secret purpose.

Three or four days later, the young men of the village

were huddled in the field opposite Sadananda's house. The village was home to some twenty-five or thirty respectable families; after sunset, the local young men gathered here for a chat, some of them sang songs, others smoked. Barring winter and the monsoon, this was where they always congregated.

Today, everyone was teasing a young man named Amrito. Somewhat eccentric in nature, Amrito was the orphaned nephew of one of the inhabitants of the village. Absurdly thin and lanky, he was rather garrulous, and forever trying to prove his courage and intelligence. Therefore, he became the butt of everyone's jokes whenever they found an opportunity.

It had begun that morning. A young man named Nadu had got married recently; his wife's name was Papia. She was on her way to fetch water from the pond, carrying a pitcher; other young women were present too. Amrito was skipping stones on the water; when he saw Nadu's wife, on an impulse he imitated the cry of the papia—the Indian nightingale—'Piu piu, pia pia papia . . .'

The young women giggled. Humiliated, the bride returned home at once and reported the incident to her husband. Flying into a rage, Nadu came running with a stick, whereupon Amrito promptly scaled a coconut tree at the edge of the water. The village elders arrived to restore peace. Everyone—even the stubborn Nadu—knew that Amrito had no evil intentions. Things didn't get out of hand.

But Amrito was not spared gibes and taunts by his friends. Everyone gathered around him as soon as he arrived at the evening haunt.

'You're such a brave man,' jeered Patal, 'but you couldn't fight with Nadu. You had to escape into a coconut tree!'

'Hmmph!' countered Amrito. 'I climbed the tree for a coconut. I'm not afraid of Nedo; if he didn't have that stick I'd have tripped him so hard he'd be groaning in bed right now.'

'Wonderful!' said Gopal. 'You got a thrashing from your uncle when you went home, didn't you?'

'Uncle didn't thrash me, he loves me.' Amrito shook his head. 'But my aunt boxed my ears—you're an ass, she said.'

Everyone chortled with glee. 'Shame on you, such a coward,' declared Patal. 'Imagine having your ears boxed by a woman.'

'She's an elder in the family, so I spared her,' answered Amrito. 'You can't act funny with me.'

'Tell me, Amra, you're not afraid of people, are you?' said Dashu. 'Now tell the truth, what do you do when you see a ghost?'

'. . . all over his clothes,' quipped someone softly.

'I have seen a ghost but I wasn't afraid,' said Amrito, looking fierce.'

'You have? When? Where?' Everyone spoke up at once.

'Over there,' responded Amrito, proudly pointing to the forest with his thin arm.

'When did you see it? What did you see?'

'A ghost horse,' answered Amrito in a solemn tone.

One or two of the listeners laughed. 'You're an ass yourself,' said Gopal, 'so no wonder you saw a ghost horse. When did you see it?'

'The night before last.' Amrito recounted the events of the night. 'Our calf Kailey had slipped out of its tether and run off from the cowshed. Go check the forest, Amra, said Uncle. It was ten at night; but I'm not afraid of anything, so off I went to the forest. I looked all over, but there was no calf anywhere. The moonlight made the place look strange—suddenly I saw a horse. The clatter of the hooves made me think I had found the calf; when I turned to look, I saw a horse disappearing in a flash in the forest. A black horse, with flames coming out of its nostrils. I went back praying. When you pray, ghosts can't do anything.'

'Which way did the ghost horse come? And which way did it go?' asked Dashu.

'It came from the direction of the village, towards the station.'

'Was anyone riding the horse?'

'I didn't see all that.'

There was silence for some time. Amrito did not have enough imagination to make up a ghost story. He must have seen a live horse. But how would a horse appear in the forest? No one in the village owned a horse. Even the American soldiers who had camped in the forest during the war did not have horses. There was a horse-drawn coach or two in the station-town, but why would those horses be cantering in the forest here at night? Had Amrito mistaken the runaway calf for a horse, then?

'I see, you mistook the calf for a ghost horse,' Patal said at last.

Amrito shook his head vehemently. 'Oh no, it was a horse. I saw a flesh-and-blood ghost horse.'

'Are you telling us you didn't faint even after seeing a ghost horse?'

'Why should I faint? I was praying.'

'Well done. But you must have been praying because you were terrified.'

'Not at all,' Amrito blustered. 'Who says I was terrified. I'm never afraid.'

'Look Amra, don't brag,' said Dashu. 'Do you dare go into the forest now?'

'Why shouldn't I?' Amrito looked at the forest in some trepidation. By that time night had set in and the moon had risen; the trees in the forest cast thick black shadows. Pausing, Amrito said, 'I can go if I want to, but why should I? There isn't a calf missing now.'

'Maybe there isn't,' said Gopal. 'But how can we be sure you weren't fibbing?'

'Fibbing!' Amrito jumped to his feet. 'Me fib! Look Gopla, you don't know me . . .'

'All right, help me know you. Let's see you go into the forest alone. Then we'll know how brave you are.'

Amrito couldn't take it any more. 'I'm going in—this moment,' he announced confidently. 'Do you think I'm scared?'

'Take this piece of chalk,' Patal called him back. 'You needn't go in too deep—just as far as the large cotton tree behind Sadananda-da's house.Leave a mark on the trunk. That'll prove you really did go in.'

Taking the chalk, Amrito asked with a slight tremor in his voice, 'All of you will be here, won't you?'

'We will.'

Amrito set off towards the forest. The further he advanced, the more he dragged his feet. Still, eventually he did disappear behind Sadananda Sur's house.

The young men sitting in the field stared in silence at the forest under the pale moonlight. One of them lit up. 'Maybe he's just lurking near Sadananda-da's house,' another one sniggered.

Some time passed. All eyes were on the forest.

Suddenly there was the sound of a crack. It came from the forest. A sound not unlike the breaking of a dry twig. The young men exchanged startled glances.

Some more time passed. But Amrito did not return. The cotton tree which was Amrito's destination was no more than fifty or sixty yards away from the spot where the young men had congregated. What was taking him so long?

After another three or four minutes, Patal stood up. 'Let's go take a look. What's keeping Amra?'

They proceeded in a group along the route that Amrito had taken. 'Do you suppose he's ridden off on the ghost horse?' remarked one of them.

But Amrito had not fled. The cotton tree was about twenty-five yards away from the back door of Sadananda Sur's house. Something white lay in the darkness pierced by the moonlight. They went closer to discover it was . . . Amrito.

One of them lit a match. Amrito lay on his back, his shirt sodden with blood at the chest.

Amrito had not died of fright; he had been shot dead.

2

Byomkesh and I were in Santalgola on an official investigation. While salaried policemen were not favourably disposed towards Byomkesh, he was highly regarded by the higher administration. Cases that the police had given up on were sometimes passed on to him.

Many foreign soldiers had set up camp in different parts of the country during the last world war; at the end of the war the foreigners left, and Indians earned the right to rule themselves. When the nation raised its head after the bloodbath of Independence, it discovered that the upper levels of the lake may be clear, but malevolent crocodiles were swimming about in its depths. The arms and ammunition that the soldiers had left behind had become the teeth and claws of these crocodiles. Rail accidents, bomb explosions, armed robberies . . . acts like these left the new administration continually harassed.

Although the police did succeed in apprehending some of the perpetrators, they had not unearthed the source of the bombs, pistols and other weapons. It was not difficult to surmise that the weapons had been stashed somewhere close to where the foreign soldiers had set up camp; but apprehending the suppliers of these arms was proving difficult. Unless the kingpins running the black market in illegal arms were caught, it would not be possible to root out this menace.

After consultations with officials, Byomkesh had decided to make Santalgola his first port of call. It was a small place, and could in no circumstances be called a city. A row of living quarters for railway employees stood near the station. A single paved road led from the station in both directions, circling back upon itself to enclose an area of some nine acres. This area held a few large warehouses, the police station, the post office, a cooperative bank, the government rest house, and so on. The two rice mills I have referred to already were situated at either end of the area encircled by the road. Although most of the inhabitants were Bengalis, there were not a small number of Hindustanis and Marwaris too.

We had set up base at the government rest house. Byomkesh had not wanted to reveal who he was; the more anonymous you can remain in such investigations, the better. But when we arrived we discovered that Byomkesh's identity and the reason for his arrival were open secrets. Sukhamay Samanta,the local police inspector, had already been briefed by his department, and Byomkesh's fame had spread in every direction thanks to his efforts.

Inspector Sukhamay's countenance was exceedingly pleasant, but he was in fact the embodiment of evil intentions. In public he assisted Byomkesh, but in private he placed as many obstacles in Byomkesh's path as he could. Perhaps he did not approve of an outsider succeeding where the police had failed.

Be that as it may, Byomkesh began his work despite the hindrances. Realizing that anonymity was impossible, he started his investigations in full view of everyone. Visiting the police station openly, he collected a list of the principal inhabitants of the area. At the railway station, he struck up an acquaintance with the stationmaster, the goods inspector, the ticket-checker and others; he made enquiries about wealthy individuals at the cooperative bank. But since everyone had come to know the purpose of his visit, there was no progress despite everyone's cooperation.

After four or five days of fruitless exploration, Byomkesh devised a strategy. He wrote an anonymous letter to each of the well-off locals who could be suspected. The substance of the letter: *I have become aware of your clandestine activities; we will meet shortly.* I took the train to a junction town a couple of stations away to post the letters.

We may have laid the bait, but there was no sign of the fish. Two or three more days passed this way. Sleeping lazily through the day and taking invigorating walks every morning and evening led to considerable improvement in health, but there was no progress when it came to work.

Then, three young men from Baghmari appeared one morning.

As we savoured a most pleasing sensation at about eight in the morning after consuming hot jalebis washed down with warm milk, the sight of three faces peeping in at the door made Byomkesh step out and ask, 'What do you want?'

The rest house comprised two adjoining rooms, with a roofed veranda in front. Having climbed up to the veranda, three young men were milling about hesitantly. They smiled widely at the sight of Byomkesh. 'Are you Byomkesh-babu?' one of them asked deferentially.

'Yes,' said Byomkesh.

The smiles stretched from ear to ear. 'We're from Baghmari village,' one of them announced.

'Baghmari! Where's that?'

'Not far, just a mile away.'

'Come in,' said Byomkesh, leading them into the room. The furniture in the rest house was standard issue—a chair, a desk, an easy chair, two beds, and a coir mat on the floor. Two of the visitors settled down on the floor, while the third perched on the desk. Stretching out in the easy chair, Byomkesh said, 'Now tell me why you are here.'

The young man who had taken the initiative to speak first was named Patal. The other two were named Dashu and Gopal. 'Haven't you heard?' asked Gopal. 'Someone's been murdered horribly in our village.'

'What! When?' Byomkesh sat up in his easy chair.

'The night before last,' Dashu and Gopal answered in unison.

'The police was informed at once,' Patal added. 'Inspector Sukhamay Samanta visited the spot yesterday at about nine in the morning. He took the corpse away, but there's been no news since then. We went to the police station before coming to you—Inspector Sukhamay threw us out. The corpse has apparently been sent to the police headquarters for a postmortem. Aren't you aware of any of this? But we were told you were here to help the police.'

'The inspector probably considered it unnecessary to inform me,' Byomkesh replied dryly. 'Never mind. Who has been killed, and by whom? What was the murder weapon?'

'The weapon was a gun. The person killed was a friend of ours—Amrito. No one knows who the murderer is. We're also partly responsible for Amra's death, Byomkesh-babu; this terrible outcome was a result of our tomfoolery. That's why we've turned to you. Inspector Sukhamay is a nincompoop; we entreat you to find the murderer. We shall be indebted to you forever.'

'Shot dead!' exclaimed Byomkesh. 'Incredible! Tell me the whole story.'

The story that Patal, Dashu and Gopal now recounted, individually and jointly, has already been told. They did not seem particularly distraught by Amrito's death, but his mysterious killing had aroused their interest. And with Byomkesh at hand, their interest now acquired melodramatic proportions.

It took about two hours to recount the story of Amrito's death; Byomkesh intervened occasionally with questions for greater clarity. 'It certainly is a mysterious affair, and a gun to top it all. But it is not enough to merely listen to your account. I must examine the spot of the murder.'

All of them grew animated. 'Why don't we go right now, Byomkesh-babu?' said Patal. 'We'll be honoured to have you visit our village.'

'Not now,' said Byomkesh, glancing at his watch. 'Since two days have gone by already, half a day more will not make any difference. We shall visit your village at about five this evening.'

'Very well, we'll come and fetch you.'

They left.

Inspector Sukhamay arrived after some time. Wedging his considerable girth into the chair, he said, 'Those rascals from Baghmari came to you, didn't they? They came to me too. Young Bengalis carried away by all the excitement—they won't give it up in a hurry. Don't pay them any attention, I tell you, or they'll make your life miserable.'

'Oh no, why should I?' answered Byomkesh. 'You know them well, don't you? Are they good boys?'

'Village boys spoilt rotten, with no work on their hands to do, that's all,' said Sukhamay-babu. 'Living off whatever little their fathers have—half an acre to grow rice on, or a couple of coconut trees.'

'The victim was part of their group too, wasn't he?' asked Byomkesh.

'Yes, he went one step better. Lived off his uncle, disgraceful behaviour.'

'I'm told he was shot dead.'

'So it seems, but nothing can be said for sure till investigations are completed.'

'Hmm. Do you suspect anyone?'

'How can I? No one saw anything; they were all huddled together in the field. But there's one person I'm suspicious about. Amrito had insulted Nadu's wife that very morning. Nadu is a hot-headed mule; he chased Amrito with a stick. He wasn't present at the evening session either. I must have him brought to the police station and softened up. But never mind all this nonsense now. I'm here to give you some important news.' Suddenly lowering his voice, he said, 'You must have heard of Jamnadas Gangaram, one of the biggest dealers hereabouts. He's received an anonymous letter.'

'An anonymous letter!' exclaimed Byomkesh, displaying intense curiosity. 'What does it say?'

'Jamnadas showed me the letter in secret,' Sukhamay-babu said. 'It came in an envelope and all it said was: "I have become aware of your clandestine activities; we will meet shortly."'

'Really! Then Jamnadas must be kept under watch.'

'But of course. I've set a man on him. He's watching Jamnadas round the clock.'

'Excellent! You're a seasoned hand, you've got it right. The case might be solved now.'

Modest self-satisfaction played over Sukhamay-babu's face. 'Hehe . . . I'm an old hand at all this, Byomkesh-babu. Still, never mind all that. Have you made any progress?'

'None,' replied Byomkesh, sounding disheartened. 'I seek, I do not find.'

Although he did not get the allusion, Sadananda-babu pretended that he had and chortled in his customary way. Prising himself out of the chair with great effort, he said, 'I'd better go now, I have a lot of work at the station.'

Byomkesh got to his feet too. 'By the way, have you received Amrito's postmortem report?'

'Not yet,' answered Sukhamay-babu, raising his eyebrows. 'In a day or two, perhaps. But why?'

'Show it to me when you do.'

'I will if you want me to,' said Sukhamay-babu, losing his good cheer. 'But you're here to catch the big fish, Byomkesh-babu, if you now turn to the small fry too how will we survive?'

'Oh no, I'm not doing that. It's pure curiosity. As they say, the idle mind is the devil's workshop.'

The smile returned to Sukhamay-babu's countenance. He noticed me for the first time on his way out. 'Ah Ajit-babu, how are you?' he said. 'Still writing? Your cock-and-bull tales aren't bad to read—hehe. But nothing like Robert Blake. Goodbye.'

When he had passed out of earshot, Byomkesh winked at me. 'Hehe,' he said.

3

The young men escorted us to their village late that afternoon. We walked along the railway line. When we arrived, every male inhabitant, down to the last old man and little boy, had gathered by the line to welcome us. Everyone's eyes bulged with curiosity. They wanted to see for themselves what kind of creature Byomkesh Bakshi was.

We entered the village as part of a procession. Patal stepped forward to lead us to one of the buildings. It was half brick house, half hut. There were two brick rooms in the front half, while the rest of the structure had a thatched roof. This was the house of the dead Amrito's uncle.

Amrito's uncle Balaram-babu had made arrangements for tea on the raised courtyard in front of the house. He welcomed us with a deferential greeting. He appeared to be a simple sort, his manner of speaking betraying both diffidence and stiffness. Although he did not seem overcome by grief at his nephew's death, he did appear flustered.

'You didn't have to,' said Byomkesh, indicating the arrangements for tea.

Slurring his words, Balaram-babu said, 'Just . . . some tea . . .'

'It is a matter of great fortune for us that you have deigned to visit our village,' declared Patal. 'You must have a cup of tea.'

'All in good time,' responded Byomkesh. 'Let me explore the forest first.'

'Come with me, please.'

Patal led us away again. Some of the other young men joined us. The unpaved path that ran past Balaram-babu's house was the main road of the village. It ended at the edge of an uneven field strewn with rocks. A single brick structure stood on the other side—Sadananda Sur's house. Behind it began the forest. We went down to the field. 'Is this where all of you had gathered that evening?'

'Yes sir.'

'Where exactly were you sitting?'

'Here . . .' Patal went further into the field. 'At this spot.'

The spot was relatively clean, free of weeds. 'Take me along the route that Amrito took into the forest,' directed Byomkesh.

'Come with me, please.'

A lock hung on Sadananda Sur's door, the windows were closed. We went around the house. At the back was a walled yard, the wall as tall as a man, with a door set in it. The denseness of trees in the forest reached all the way to the door.

We entered the forest at the back of the house. The trees had started shedding their leaves, the branches were bare; the ground was covered with a layer of wizened yellowing leaves. An enormous cotton tree stood twenty-five or thirty yards behind the back door, its pillar-like trunk rising eleven or twelve feet into the air before branching out in different directions. Leading us to a spot beneath the tree, Patal pointed to the ground. 'This is where Amrito lay dead.'

The area was smothered in fallen leaves and cotton flowers, without the slightest sign of an unnatural death having taken place. Still Byomkesh searched the ground carefully. There were no marks on the hard surface—all he found was a piece of chalk under the dry leaves. Holding it aloft, Byomkesh said, 'Amrito had brought this piece of chalk to make a mark on the tree. But this tree has no mark. Therefore . . .'

'Yes sir,' said Patal, 'even before he could . . .'

There was nothing more to see here. We turned back. On the way back Byomkesh said, 'Let me check whether Sadananda Sur's back door is closed.'

Pushing on the door, we discovered it was latched inside. There were holes in the ancient planks on the door. Peeping through one we discovered a small shrine inside, while the rest of the yard was overrun with weeds. A guava tree grew in one corner. There was nothing else to catch our eye.

Byomkesh proceeded to walk back, skirting the wall, his eyes on the ground. 'What's that?' he said, suddenly pointing to something at the corner of the wall.

A half moon-shaped mark was clearly visible on the bare, dry earth; around it were a few wavering, indistinct scratches. Byomkesh stooped to examine the marks, as did we. Looking up, he observed the branches of the guava tree that were visible across the wall.

'What are you looking at?' I asked. 'What are those marks?'

'What do you think?' Byomkesh asked Patal.

Patal turned pale; licking his lips, he said, 'They look like the hoofmarks of a horse.'

'Yes, the hoofmarks of the ghost horse,' remarked Byomkesh. 'So Amrito was not lying.'

We walked back. Byomkesh's brow remained furrowed with doubt. He was confronted by a mystery, for he had as yet been unable to comprehend the significance of the hoofmark. We barely exchanged a word or two on the way back. 'How long has Sadananda Sur been away?' asked Byomkesh.

'About seven or eight days,' answered Patal.

'Did he say when he'd be back?'

'No.'

'And no one knows where he has gone?'

'No.'

Returning to Balaram-babu's house, we took our seats. The crowd of onlookers had thinned, but three or four eager individuals were still milling about in the hope of catching a glimpse of Byomkesh. Balaram-babu fetched tea and snacks for us. Patal, Dashu, Gopal and the other young men hovered over us in supervision.

Over tea, Byomkesh began interrogating Balaram-babu.

'Was Amrito your sister's son? Not a cousin's?'

'My sister's, yes.'

'Are his parents dead?'

'Yes. My sister was widowed when Amrito was a baby. She used to live in my house. Then she died too. Amrito was five.'

'You do not have children of your own?'

'I have a daughter. She is married.'

'How old was Amrito?'

'Twenty-one.'

'You did not arrange for his marriage?'

'No. He was a bit soft in the head, so I didn't.'

'Did he have a job?'

'Now and then, but he couldn't stick to it. I had got him a job with Bhagabati-babu, one of the biggest traders in Santalgola; he even worked there for some time. Then he worked for a month or so at the Marwari Badridas' rice mill, but Badridas dismissed him as well. Of late he was frequenting Bishu Mallik's rice mill, but he hadn't got a job.'

Byomkesh munched on a savoury for a few minutes, then suddenly asked after a sip of tea, 'Does anyone in the village own a horse?'

Balaram-babu's eyes began to protrude, while the young men exchanged glances. 'No one in the village owns a horse,' Balaram-babu answered eventually.

'Anyone have a gun-licence?'

'No, sir.'

'I've been told of a young man named Nadu, I don't know what his full name is. I'd like to ask him a question or two.'

Balaram-babu looked at the young men, who exchanged glances again. Then Patal said, 'Nadu left for his wife's parents' house with her yesterday.'

'Where do they live?'

'In Kailashpur. You have to take a train; it's three or four stations from Santalgola.'

Byomkesh finished his tea, lost in thought. Nadu may have been innocent, but why had he fled? Was he afraid? Not surprising—who would not be apprehensive if their name were dragged into a murder?

Suddenly one of the young men said, 'There's Sadananda-da.'

We turned our heads as one. A gentleman was approaching along the road. Although he looked rustic, his attire was far from rustic; he was dressed in a silk kurta and a warm shawl, with burnished shoes on his feet and a canvas bag in his hand.

'Have you seen how nattily Sadananda-da's dressed?' whispered one of the young men to another. 'He must have been to Calcutta.'

As he was passing us, Patal called out, 'Have you heard what's happened, Sadananda-da?'

Sadananda-babu stopped, observed Byomkesh and me, and asked, 'What's happened?'

'Amra's died,' answered Patal.

'Died!' Unadulterated surprise surfaced in Sadananda-babu's eyes. 'Died of what?'

'He wasn't ill,' Patal told him. 'He was shot dead. No one knows who killed him.'

Sadananda-babu's face turned to stone, he stared fixedly. 'You'd better go home now since you've only just arrived, you can hear the whole story later,' Patal said.

Sadananda-babu hesitated for a few moments before proceeding on his way slowly.

After he had disappeared from sight, Byomkesh asked Patal, 'Didn't Sadananda-babu have a canvas bag and a steel trunk when he left?'

'You're right,' replied Patal, 'that's what Hiru the headman had said. Where did he leave his trunk?'

No one had a suitable answer. Looking around him, Byomkesh rose to his feet. 'It's getting on for evening, we'll be on our way now. It would have helped to have had a word with Sadananda-babu, but he's only just returned . . .'

Before Byomkesh could finish, a loud explosion shook us momentarily. Then Byomkesh leapt on to the road and raced towards Sadananda Sur's house. We followed. That was where the sound had come from.

Arriving at Sadananda Sur's house, we discovered that the main door had collapsed on the front terrace, on which lay Sadananda Sur's blood-soaked body. The stench of gunpowder was spreading on the evening breeze.

4

Byomkesh and I climbed on the terrace, while those following us gathered at one corner and stared in round-eyed silence.

It was clear at a glance that Sadananda Sur was no longer alive. It was true that his body was relatively untouched; his right hand still firmly gripped the lock, and his left hand, the key. But his head had been almost entirely severed from his body and twisted backwards, a mixture of blood and grey matter oozing from his crushed skull, and one side of his face was missing altogether. It was a gruesome sight. To think that someone who was alive even three minutes ago was now in this condition made one tremble in nervous trepidation—the limbs ran cold.

The villagers had been speechless all this while. Patal was the first to regain his voice. 'What's going on in our village, Byomkesh-babu!' he asked, his voice shaking.

Byomkesh was examining a piece of welded iron near the shattered door—he probably didn't hear Patal. Tossing the piece of iron aside, he said, 'Hand grenade! Where's the canvas bag gone?'

The bag lay in shreds on one side. Going up to it, Byomkesh examined its interiors. There were some garments, old and new. A new table clock had been flattened by the explosion, while a bottle of hair-oil had been broken, leaving the clothes sodden. There was nothing else.

'Stay here, Ajit,' Byomkesh told me. 'I'll take a quick look inside the house.'

Not only had the panels of the door collapsed, the arch above the door had also been blown off, leaving several bricks precariously suspended. I couldn't contain myself when Byomkesh entered through this opening on slow footsteps. Who knew where in this accursed house a ghastly death was lying in wait? If something were to happen to Byomkesh, how would I face Satyabati?

'I'm coming too,' I said, taking my life in my hands and following him in.

Turning his head, Byomkesh smiled. 'There's nothing to be afraid of,' he said. 'The threat is now gone, just like Sadananda Sur himself.'

It was getting dark meanwhile, and the light inside the house was dim. 'Take a look at whatever you need to quickly. It's getting dark,' I said.

There were two rooms in the front half of the house, while the kitchen was at the back. None of the rooms held anything of interest. The room whose door had been shattered contained only a broken bedstead; in the next room, the mattress and pillows on another cot made it clear that this was the master's bedroom. There was nothing besides a few dirty clothes in a cupboard set in the wall, its doors open.

The kitchen was in the same state. There were a few plates and glasses, pots and pitchers, and cooking utensils. The clay oven was dirty too, ash heaped inside it. 'Sadananda Sur did not seem to have been particularly well off,' I observed.

'Hmm,' said Byomkesh. 'Did you notice that door?' He pointed at the door.

I went up to it for a closer look. The kitchen door led into the backyard. It was shut, but opened at a touch. 'What!' I exclaimed. 'The door was open!'

'Sadananda Sur hadn't left it open,' said Byomkesh. 'He had latched it. Check carefully.'

When I looked closely, I found the latch hanging on one

side, but it was barely a few inches long. 'How can it be so small?' I asked.

'Don't you see?' answered Byomkesh. 'The latch was of the regular size and in place. Then someone parted the door from outside and sawed it open to enter the room. There's the rest of the latch.' Byomkesh pointed to where the remaining portion lay amidst the kindling next to the oven.

Although I understood some of it, the entire affair grew murkier. An enemy of Sadananda Sur's had sawed through the latch to enter the door in his absence. And then? How did the bomb explode today? Who had made it explode?

We stepped into the backyard through the open door. A draw-well was located in one corner of the walled yard, and a guava tree in the other. Byomkesh went directly to the tree and examined the soil beneath it. Although I was unable to draw any conclusions from the faint scruff marks on the ground, Byomkesh nodded. 'Hmm, just as I suspected. This is where the intruder jumped over the wall.'

'Really?' I asked. 'But why did he have to jump over the wall? Why didn't he saw his way through the back door as well?'

'If he had done that the back door would have stayed open, and someone may have noticed,' said Byomkesh. 'That would have made things difficult for the intruder. I misinterpreted the whole thing at the outset, else Sadananda Sur would not have had to die.'

'What did you misinterpret?'

'I had suspected Sadananda Sur of being the person I was here to apprehend. But I was wrong. Let us go. There's nothing else to see in Baghmari.'

We walked back through the kitchen to the front door. Meanwhile, the entire village had gathered, huddling together beneath the terrace to stare at the corpse. People's curiosity about death is infinite.

Patal spoke up from the crowd. 'What did you see in the house, Byomkesh-babu? Did you find anyone?'

'No,' answered Byomkesh. 'Have you informed the police?'

'No,' replied Patal. 'Since you're here . . .'

'I'm no one, it's the police you have to inform,' declared Byomkesh. 'But never mind, you needn't go; we were leaving in any case, we shall inform Sukhamay-babu on our way.'

'You're leaving?'

'Yes. Some of you must wait here till the police arrive.'

'Will the police arrive tonight?'

'They will.'

Once again we walked along the railway line. The moon was about to break through the darkness. A goods train panted past us, dragging its long, weighed-down body.

'You appear to have unravelled part of the mystery, Byomkesh,' I remarked. 'But I am completely in the dark.'

Byomkesh didn't answer for some time. Then he said, 'I'm sure you've realized that there is a very close connection between the deaths of Amrito and Sadananda Sur.'

'Is there? What connection?'

'Poor Amrito died unknowingly,' Byomkesh sighed. 'Had he not wandered into the forest that night he would not have died. The person who killed him had not intended to kill him.'

'Then whom did he intend to kill?'

'Sadananda Sur.'

'But . . . Sadananda Sur wasn't home at the time.'

'It was because he was not that the assailant had come to kill him.'

'This is all very mysterious. As the saying goes, presence of mind is better than absence of body. Anyway, how did the bomb explode today?'

Lighting a cigarette, Bymokesh blew a smoke ring and asked, 'Do you know what a booby trap is?'

'I've heard of the term,' I replied.

'Someone had wanted to murder Sadananda Sur. When he came to know Sadananda Sur was away, he climbed over the wall one evening, sawed through the latch and entered the house, then balanced a bomb over the closed front door so that it would explode when the door was opened. Sadananda Sur opened the door on his return today, and the bomb exploded at once. Do you see now?'

'I do. But who's the man?'

'I do not know his name yet. But he deals in black market for weapons and rides to war on a black horse in the evening. I am also desirous of knowing his name and whereabouts.'

When we reached Santalgola, the buzz of activity had

quietened down, with most of the shops having closed. The police station was open—Sukhamay-babu was at his desk, poring over documents. Raising his eyes at the sound of our footsteps, he asked, 'Any news?'

'Serious news,' answered Byomkesh. 'There's been another murder at Baghmari.'

'Murder!' Sukhamay jumped to his feet.

'Yes. Do you know Sadananda Sur?'

'I may have seen him, I can't quite remember. Has Sadananda Sur been murdered? And how did you find out before anyone else?'

'I was at Baghmari.'

The mask of geniality slipped from Sukhamay-babu's face for a moment; with a hostile look, he said, 'You went to Baghmari. Despite my forbidding you to.'

Byomkesh gave him a piercing glance. 'Who are you to forbid me?'

'I am the senior inspector of this area, the head of the police,' Sukhamay-babu retorted brusquely.

'You could be the Lord Almighty of the police force for all I care, but you are no one to issue orders to me,' Byomkesh responded. 'I am here on behalf of the government, Inspector Samanta. You have been ordered to cooperate with me in every possible way. But far from helping, you are trying to hinder me at every step. But I am warning you, one more false move from you and you shall be forced to abandon this area. You might even have to abandon your job.'

Sukhamay-babu may have thrown his weight about

earlier under the impression that Byomkesh was harmless. But now, when he saw Byomkesh's real self, he shrank. His mask of affability returned in an instant. Pouring his inherent servility into his voice, he said, 'I lost my head. Forgive me, Byomkesh-babu. I have a stomachache since this evening, I don't know what I'm saying. Me order you! How can you say such a thing. I am your servant, at your beck and call. Hehe. So it is Sadananda Sur who has been murdered?'

Byomkesh had not calmed down yet. 'You did not investigate Amrito's murder the night that you were informed,' he said. 'You did not go to the spot until the next morning. I am sure you are aware of what the outcome would be were your superiors to be told of this.'

'How do I explain, Byomkesh-babu,' pleaded Sukhamay-babu in distress, 'I had the colic that evening too, hehe, it was tearing me apart. Not going to the murder spot would have been out of the question otherwise. Now Sadananda Sur . . . I'm leaving at once. Come here, constable. Get them to prepare my horse. And you get ready too. There's been a big murder. We have to go immediately.'

Since Sukhamay-babu was about to ride off, dressed for war, we left. The police had to cover long distances in the countryside for their investigations, which was probably why they were equipped with horses.

5

'Let us walk up to the station,' Byomkesh proposed after breakfast the next morning. The last train had left at seven in the morning, the next one was due in two hours. There was neither any crowd at the station, nor a ticket-checker at the entrance. Everyone except the stationmaster Haribilash-babu had probably taken the opportunity to retire to their respective quarters for a cup of tea.

We had met Haribilash-babu already. His disposition was grave, and his appearance suggested a permanently bad stomach. His statements were measured, and he thought twice before uttering a word. Despite our acquaintance, we had not conversed at length. When we began to stroll aimlessly on the deserted platform, he emerged from his office to observe us silently over the rims of his spectacles.

Byomkesh, of course, was not there to merely stroll on the platform; he was there to gather information. However, he did not approach Haribilash-babu. Extracting information from him and excavating the depths of a mine for precious stones were equally arduous. But if anyone else were to arrive instead . . .

We did not have to wait long. Monotosh the ticket-checker, who had probably spotted us from his quarters, arrived on the platform, wiping his face. He was a quick-witted young man with the gift of the gab. 'What a to-do. Imagine it all happening before your very eyes!'

'I see you've heard,' responded Byomkesh.

'Of course we have. We heard even before the 10:17 had entered the station last night. What was it that you saw? Did the bomb explode right under your nose?'

'Not exactly under my nose, but definitely under my ears,' said Byomkesh. 'Did you know Sadananda Sur?'

'Of course I did! He got off the 4:53, handed me his ticket and was leaving with his bag when I said—I see you've been to Calcutta, dada; did you see the sights? Laughing, he said, do you think Calcutta is for seeing the sights? I saw the nights. He left, laughing. Who knew he wouldn't be alive half an hour later.'

After a moment's thought Byomkesh asked, 'Did you see Sadananda Sur leaving?'

'Of course I did,' answered Monotosh. 'Do you think anyone can leave this station without my knowledge? It happened eight days ago; he showed me his ticket and entered the station in the morning, leaving by the 7:03 Down.'

'Was his ticket for Calcutta?'

'Er, I don't quite remember. But where else could it have been for?'

'It could have been for a different station. Anyway. Can you tell me what luggage he had?'

'Luggage!' Scratching his head, Monotosh said, 'As far as I can remember, he had a canvas bag in one hand and a steel trunk in the other. But why?'

'Sadananda-babu didn't bring the trunk back. Which means he left it somewhere. I see you knew him quite well. What kind of a person was he?'

'I can't say. I'm in the dark there. But he was a polite gentleman. He never meddled in other people's affairs, kept himself to himself. A month or so ago he used to be a regular at the stationmaster's office.'

'Indeed. Why?'

'I have no idea. No one but they can tell you what they used to whisper over. Why don't you ask the stationmaster?'

'Yes, I think I will.'

We went up to Haribilash-babu's cabin. 'May we come in?' asked Byomkesh.

Haribilash-babu looked at us with raised eyebrows, his manner suggesting he had no idea who we were. Then, putting his pen down with a display of annoyance at being interrupted at his work, he said, 'Very well, come in.'

Entering, we took our seats. The stationmaster and we sat on opposite sides of an enormous desk weighed down by countless notebooks and documents. 'You have probably heard that Sadananda Sur has died,' said Byomkesh.

Examining the question with deep suspicion, Haribilash-babu replied, 'I have.'

'Did you know him?' asked Byomkesh.

'Slightly,' responded Haribilash-babu, having pondered deeply over the question, as though it were a matter of life or death.

'Look, please do not assume that I am questioning you out of sheer inquisitiveness,' said Byomkesh a little testily. 'Sadananda-babu died a particularly horrifying death, and I am investigating this case on behalf of the police. Now tell me how you came to be acquainted with Sadananda-babu.'

Haribilash-babu's face with its already sunken cheeks collapsed further. After clearing his throat a couple of times, he began to speak rather hesitantly. 'Sadananda Sur's brother-in-law Prankeshta Pal is a line-inspector with the Railways. I knew him already. He was posted to this line a few months ago; his headquarters are at Ramdihi Junction. It is his responsibility to inspect the line, for which he travels up and down in a trolley. He travels through Santalgola quite often in the course of his work, which is how I happened to meet him. One day, Sadananda-babu arrived while Prankeshta-babu and I were talking on the platform. Prankeshta-babu introduced us, explaining the relationship between them. That was when I came to be acquainted with Sadananda-babu.'

Byomkesh's eyes narrowed as he listened; he asked, 'How long ago did this meeting take place?'

'About two or three months ago.'

'Prankeshta-babu was a regular on this line. When was he here last?'

'Four or five days ago. He didn't linger at the station; he went off on the trolley on his inspection.'

'Were the brothers-in-law on good terms with each other?'

'I cannot speak for what lay within, but on the surface they were.'

'Anyway. Sadananda Sur used to visit you thereafter. With what objective?'

After another bout of careful consideration in silence,

Haribilash-babu said, 'Sadananda-babu was an agent, he used to deal in this and that. Observing my dyspepsia, he was cajoling with me to try Ayurvedic treatment. He had managed to sell me a couple of medicines too; ginger and saltpetre. Useless.'

Oh dear, ginger and saltpetre! But Byomkesh persisted. 'There was nothing else that you discussed?'

'No.'

'I have troubled you needlessly,' sighed Byomkesh, getting to his feet. 'Is Prankeshta-babu still posted at Ramdihi Junction?'

'He is.'

'Goodbye. Come, Ajit.'

'Now what?' I asked when we had left the station.

'We must pay a visit to Prankeshta-babu at Ramdihi this evening. Even if he has not heard of his brother-in-law's death yet, he will have by then. What did you make of Haribilash-babu?'

'You can certainly judge this book by its cover,' I said. 'His intelligence is as rusted as his appearance is termite-eaten. A double lock on an empty chest. If you suspect him of selling arms and ammunition on the sly in the black market, you can abandon that notion. Haribilash-babu's only bullets are his chunks of ginger, and his only gunpowder is his saltpetre.'

Byomkesh smiled. 'Let us walk over to the market,' he said.

'Are you planning to buy something?'

'Come and see.'

The hubbub had begun. Bullock carts jostled one another in the clearings opposite each of the warehouses, a couple of horse-drawn wagons were among them too. Cries of 'one is one and two is two' rose from each of the warehouses. Heaped piles of rice were being weighed on scales.

A young Bengali was supervising the activities at one of the warehouses. 'Isn't this Nafar Kundu's warehouse?' Byomkesh asked, going up to him.

The young man probably recognized Byomkesh. 'Yes sir,' he answered deferentially. 'I'm his nephew.'

'Excellent,' said Byomkesh. 'And where is Kundu-babu?'

'Uncle isn't here, sir, he's gone out,' he responded. 'Did you need something?'

'Not especially. Where has he gone?'

'He didn't say, sir.'

'Indeed. When did he leave?'

'Last Tuesday evening.'

Byomkesh looked at me out of the corner of his eye. I remembered that it was last Monday that I had been to Ramdihi station to post the anonymous letters. The letters had arrived in due course on Tuesday. One of the anonymous letters had been addressed to Nafar Kundu. Had the bird flown the coop on receiving the letter, then? Was Nafar Kundu our unknown bird? Be that as it may, his young nephew didn't seem to be in the know; he was answering all the questions innocently.

'You probably do not know when he will be back, do you?'

'No sir, he didn't say.'

After some thought, Byomkesh asked, 'Did Nafarbabu receive a letter on the morning of the day on which he left?'

'Like every day, he received three or four letters that day too.'

'Hmm.'

About to leave, Byomkesh turned back. 'How many horses do you have here?'

'Horses!' said the young man in surprise.

'Yes, horses. To pull the wagons.' Byomkesh pointed to the adjoining warehouse.

Getting the drift, the young man said, 'Oh I see. No, we don't have horse-drawn wagons, we send our material on bullock carts.'

A uniformed constable arrived at this point, clicked his heels, saluted, and said, 'The inspector has requested your company.'

'Coming,' answered Byomkesh, frowning.

6

The police station was close by. On our way there, Byomkesh said, 'Did you notice what a rogue Inspector Sukhamay is? He sent his constable in full public view, so that no one is left in any doubt about my close relationship with the police.'

'Hmm. But why the summons?'

'Amrito's postmortem report has probably arrived.'

As soon as we set foot in the police station, the honey began to flow from Inspector Sukhamay's tongue. 'Welcome,

Byomkesh-babu, welcome, Ajit-babu. Do sit down. Sit here on this chair, Byomkesh-babu. I was about to call on you, but here you are instead. Hehe, here's Amrito's postmortem report. I marvel at your acumen; you were absolutely right, he was indeed killed by a bullet.' He handed the doctor's report to Byomkesh.

This Sukhamay-babu was a strange creature. We have all encountered such creatures and enviously admired them, but we have been unable to love them. They are to be found not just in the police department, but in all walks of life.

'I see the bullet was found in the body,' said Byomkesh, having read the report. 'Where is it?'

'Here you are!' Extracting a small piece of lead from a numbered tin, Sukhamay-babu handed it to Byomkesh.

Placing the bullet on his palm, Byomkesh-babu inspected it from some time before asking Sukhamay, 'What do you make of it?'

'Well, it's obviously a pistol or revolver bullet,' answered Sukhamay-babu. 'Is there anything else to make of it?'

'Of course there is,' averred Byomkesh. 'The bullet shows that it came from a .38 Automatic, the kind that American soldiers used during the war. Therefore . . .' Byomkesh paused.

'Therefore there is a link between the person who murdered Amrito and the person you are hunting for,' said Sukhamay-babu. 'In fact, they may even be the same person. Am I right?'

'I'd better not say anything,' responded Byomkesh,

returning the bullet. 'Your task is to apprehend Amrito's murderer, which you shall pursue. My task is different.'

'Of course, of course. By the way, I've dispatched Sadananda Sur's corpse to the hospital. I will show you the report as soon as it arrives.'

'There is no need to show me the report. This is your case too, I do not wish to interfere. I'm in search of the big fish, I don't care to waste my time on small fry.'

'But of course,' declared Sukhamay-babu, his eyes radiating sly amusement. 'But Byomkesh-babu, when you draw the big fish into your net, my small fry will be trapped too. I won't have to cast my own net. Hehehehe. Going already? Goodbye then.'

We left. Byomkesh looked at me and chuckled. There was no end to the inspector's cunning, and yet you couldn't help being amused by his antics. 'It's not too hot yet, let's visit the rice mills,' suggested Byomkesh.

It took five minutes to walk down the road to Bishwanath Rice Mill. It was quite a large mill, occupying some two acres of land, fenced in by barbed wire. The first thing to catch the eye on entering through the front gate, guarded by a Gurkha, was an enormous paved courtyard. Beyond the courtyard lay a reservoir, with an engine-room on the left and a shed with a corrugated roof for husking the paddy; on the right lay the warehouse, the office and a row of rooms in which the owner lived. The morning's activities had begun, as a crackling sound from the paddy-husking shed indicated. The labourers were busy at work, sacks were being loaded on and unloaded from bullock carts and horse-drawn wagons.

The owner of the rice mill was named Bishwanath Mallik. Despite gathering his name from the police station and sending him an anonymous letter, we had not actually set eyes on him yet. Having sent a message through the Gurkha, we entered the mill. Arriving at the office, we discovered that Bishwanath-babu was not there; only a man with the appearance of a clerk was seated on the traditional mattress from which business was conducted, writing the books.

'What do you want?'

'Is Bishwanath-babu in? We're here from the police.'

Alarmed, he quickly said, 'Please come in, please take a seat. Sir is supervising mill work, he'll be here any moment. Should I send word to him?'

We sat down on the mattress, which covered half the floor. To tell the truth, such old-fashioned mattresses were far more comfortable than modern sofas and chairs. Pulling a well-stuffed bolster towards himself, Byomkesh said, 'Oh no, there's no need. I only have a couple of questions, which you can answer just as well. You're the bookkeeper, aren't you?'

Rubbing his hands in deference, the man said, 'Yes, I'm the chief accountant here. Your servant's name is Nilkantha Adhikari. And you are Byomkesh Bakshi?'

Byomkesh nodded, smiling. Nilkantha gazed at him with eyes brimming with devotion. There are people whose hearts melt at the mention of the police. On top of that, when such people hear Byomkesh Bakshi's name, their emotions surge like the waters of a flood breaching a dam; they simply cannot be contained. Nilkantha Adhikari was such a man. His expression revealed that there was nothing he could not do for Byomkesh; he was determined to answer questions, in fact, he would answer even without being questioned.

'You look like a capable man,' said Byomkesh. 'Do you look after everything at the mill yourself?'

Rubbing his hands in glee, Byomkesh said, 'Sir looks after things too. In his absence the entire responsibility falls on me.'

'Doesn't Bishwanath-babu live here?'

'He does. But when there isn't too much work at the mill, he goes to Calcutta for a few days. Sir's family lives in Calcutta.'

'I see. How long has it been since he went to Calcutta?'

'About a month. There's a lot of work now . . .'

'Very well, never mind all that. Did you know the young man named Amrito from Baghmari who died recently?'

'Of course I did,' answered Nilkantha eagerly. 'Amrito used to visit sir quite often in search of a job. But . . .'

'Did you know Sadananda Sur too?'

'I heard this morning that Sadananda-babu died last night in a bomb explosion. I used to know him very well. He was a regular visitor here.'

'With what objective?'

'Objective? He was close to sir. He used to sit here sometimes, smoke a little, chat with sir. No other objective. But . . .' Nilkantha paused.

'So he was a courtier. But what?'

'He had borrowed some money from sir about ten days ago.'

'Really! How much?'

'Five hundred.'

'Did he write a hand note when he borrowed the money?'

'No. Sir used to trust Sadananda-babu; it was put down as a loan to him in the books of accounts. The money's probably gone.' Nilkantha shook his head regretfully.

Byomkesh began to ponder, his face resting in his palm. I had no idea what he was musing on, but a little later, the neighing of a horse outside shook him out of his reverie. 'By the way, I spotted several horses here,' he said, raising his eyes. 'Are they all yours?'

'Yes, they're all ours,' Nilkantha responded with enthusiasm. 'Sir loves horses. We have nine of them.'

'Indeed. What do all these horses do? Do they pull wagons?'

'Of course they do. Besides, sir himself loves riding. He was a jockey when he was young, you see . . .'

'Nilkantha!'

From somewhere behind us, the sound landed like a

whiplash on Nilkantha's mouth. He fell silent with a terrified expression, while both of us turned our heads.

A man stood at the door. He was about forty years of age, short and slim, with large eyes sitting on a gaunt face. Although his body, clad in shorts and a half-sleeved shirt, had no deformities, his legs were curved like a bow. There was no doubt that this was the owner of the mill, the former jockey Bishwanath Mallik.

Bishwanath Mallik was still staring at Nilkantha, without having cast a single glance in our direction. Stepping into the room, he told Nilkantha as sharply as before, 'There's a delivery to the station, look after it.'

Nilkantha galloped out of the room like a whipped horse.

Finally Bishwanath Mallik turned towards us. The gravity of ownership dissipated slightly from his face, and the hint of a smile appeared. 'Nilkantha talks too much,' he said in an unruffled tone. 'Was he telling you stories about my being a jockey earlier?'

'The subject of your being a jockey came up from a discussion on horses,' said Byomkesh defensively.

'Everyone wants to bury their embarrassing past,' smiled Bishwanath. 'But I am not embarrassed. On the contrary, I regret having given up my life as a jockey, for I may have been a Khim Singh or a Khade by now. But never mind all that. You're Byomkesh-babu, aren't you? Are you here to enquire into Sadananda Sur's death? Come, let's go to my chamber.'

7

Bishu Mallik's private chamber was neatly furnished in modern style with a desk and chairs. After we took our seats he fetched a tin of cigarettes from his drawer.

Bishu Mallik may have been frail of build, but his conduct revealed a confident personality. Nor was it difficult to perceive the alert and powerful intelligence sparkling in his eyes. He lit his own cigarette after lighting ours, then sat down behind his desk. 'I know why you're in Santalgola, Byomkesh-babu,' he said. 'Possibly everyone here knows. Now tell me how I can help you. Of course, Nilkantha has told you everything about me already. If you consider me a suspect in the weapons case, you're free to search my mill, I have no objection.'

'We'll talk about searching later,' smiled Byomkesh. 'For now, please satiate my personal curiosity on one point. Why did you give up a career as a jockey to start a rice mill? So far as I know, being a jockey is lucrative.'

'It's lucrative, yes, but there are too many rules in the jockey's life, Byomkesh-babu,' Bishu-babu answered. 'You have to stay half-fed for fear of gaining weight. There are other demands too. It wasn't my cup of tea. I opened this mill before the war with my savings. And now, touchwood, it's not doing too badly.'

'But you couldn't give up on your love for horses,' responded Byomkesh. 'I see you've got several horses here as well.'

'Yes,' answered Bishu-babu with fervour. 'I love horses.

No animal is as intelligent and loyal. If man does have a genuine best friend, it's the horse and not the dog.'

'That's true,' mused Byomkesh. 'I prefer horses to dogs too. Horses come in so many different colours—red, white, black. Although you see more of red horses than white or black ones in our country. Take Santalgola—so many horses here, but I'm yet to see a single one that's black or white.'

'You're right,' said Bishu-babu. 'There isn't a single white horse hereabouts. But there is in fact a black one. It belongs to Badridas the Marwari.'

'Badridas? Who's that?'

'There's another rice mill here, owned by Badridas Giridharilal. He has several horses, one of which is black.'

Byomkesh stubbed his cigarette out in an ashtray. 'So there *is* a black horse hereabouts,' he said disinterestedly, as though his curiosity had died. 'Anyway, to get to the point. I'm not going to waste time asking for information I've got from your employee already. You have heard about Sadananda Sur's death. Coincidentally, I was in Baghmari at the time. A horrific death.'

'I was told he died in a bomb explosion,' said Bishu-babu. 'Did you see it?'

Briefly describing the manner of the death, Byomkesh added, 'Now it is not just Sadananda Sur's death but also the matter of the bomb that has to be investigated. You are an intelligent man; you can help me considerably in this business.'

'How may I be of assistance?'

'You have lived here a long time, you know the ins and outs of this place. You were here when the American soldiers were camping in this area. Can you name the people who used to frequent their tents?'

Bishu-babu pondered for a few minutes, his eyes closed. Then he said, 'I cannot say whether anyone frequented the American soldiers' camp, but they were to be seen everywhere. They were extremely sociable, they even visited my mill several times.'

'Hmm. Did they try to sell their weapons to you?'

'They did,' Bishu-babu smiled grimly. 'A sergeant had attempted to sell me a pistol. I did not purchase it.'

'You may not have, but someone else did. The question is, who was it? Can you hazard a guess?'

'Not at all. I would have informed you long ago if I could, Byomkesh-babu.'

Byomkesh pondered in silence for a while. 'Another thing. Where do you think someone would hide lethal weapons in a small place like Santalgola?'

After some more thought behind closed eyes, Bishu-babu replied, 'You're convinced that the weapons are still in Santalgola. But that may not be the case.'

'Let us assume they are.'

'Very well. But I have no idea about the size of the weapons, or the number of guns and the number of bombs. How can I identify a hiding place? If the police were to search every house, every depot and every rice mill here, they might unearth them.'

Byomkesh shook his head. 'How can that be possible? And even if it were possible, consider this. The person who has done this is not foolish enough to have hidden the arms where the police can find them easily. If the man had been so imprudent, he would have been apprehended much earlier.'

'What do you think, then?' enquired Bishu-babu eagerly. 'Where could he have hidden them?'

Byomkesh answered slowly after a pause, 'He has hidden them somewhere where no one is forbidden to go, yet where no one goes. Where, even if the stash of arms is found, it cannot be proved who has put them there.'

'Meaning . . . ?' asked Bishu-babu, his eyes bulging.

'Meaning that forest,' answered Byomkesh, pointing though the open window at the back. 'It is not particularly difficult to bury pistols and hand grenades amidst the bushes and bramble over there, but they will be impossible to find. And even if you do unearth them, how will you prove who had buried them?'

'You're right,' responded Bishu-babu enthusiastically. 'The possibility of the forest had not occurred to me. They must be buried somewhere in there.'

'Of course, I may be mistaken too,' said Byomkesh. 'But whether I have made a mistake needs to be examined.'

'No, Byomkesh-babu, you're right,' declared Bishu-babu. 'The forest should be searched without further delay.'

'That is indeed what we have to do,' agreed Byomkesh. 'But the forest is not small, searching it will take time. It might need a lot of people too. There's no time today, but tomorrow . . .'

Byomkesh stopped. He had thrown caution to the winds all this time, now he appeared to control himself; after a short, sharp look at Bishu-babu, he said, 'I have trusted you today with several pieces of information that must not get out. I told you because you're trustworthy. I hope you will not betray my trust.'

'You may rest assured that none of this shall escape my lips,' responded Bishu-babu. 'Oh, are you leaving?'

'Yes, we had better go now. I want to visit the Marwari—what did you say his name was? Ah yes, Badridas—Badridas' mill. Let me see if I can extract some information from him. I have to visit Ramdihi this evening; that is where Sadananda Sur's brother-in-law lives. By the way, did Sadananda Sur tell you why he needed the five hundred rupees he had borrowed from you?'

'He wanted to open an Ayurvedic medicine shop hereabouts,' said Bishu-babu. 'But he didn't have enough capital, which is why he asked me for a loan. Although poor, he was a decent man, which was why I lent him the money. I'm sure he would have returned the loan had he been alive, but . . . ! Never mind, I'm not losing sleep over such a small sum. I was only wondering who killed a man as harmless as Sadananda-babu. And why? Did he have a secret life then? Was his visible self not his real one?'

'Perhaps,' responded Byomkesh. 'These things are not clear yet. Maybe the meeting with his brother-in-law this evening will reveal details of his real nature. Goodbye now, we shall meet again.'

Byomkesh came back from the door, going up to Bishu-babu to tell him softly, 'I forgot to ask you something. Have you received an anonymous letter recently?'

Bishu-babu looked up, startled. 'I have. How did you know?'

'One or two others have got them too, so I thought you might have as well. What does the anonymous letter say? Does it threaten you?'

'Here you are,' said Bishu-babu, opening his drawer to extract the letter we had ourselves written.'

Byomkesh read the letter carefully before handing it back. 'Hmm. Any clue as to who the writer might be?'

'None,' replied Bishu-babu. 'I have no secrets in my life that anyone can exploit for profit.'

'Do you have any enemies?'

'Many. Everyone is an enemy of the businessman.'

'Then one of them may have written this just to create mischief. Goodbye. Many thanks.'

'So you're not searching my mill?' Bishu-babu smiled.

'Why waste time, Bishwanath-babu?' Byomkesh smiled too.

'And the forest?'

'Not today—combing the forest will need a lot of preparation. Come, Ajit, it's getting hotter. We have to be getting back after a quick chat with Badridas the Marwari.'

8

But the conversation with Badridas the Marwari provided no joy.

There are usually two kinds of appearances among Marwaris. The first, short and squat, like a duck; the second, tall and thin, like a crane. Badridas belonged to the second group. The structure of his rice mill was like Bishu-babu's; the same floor for drying the rice, the same reservoir, the same Gurkha doorman at the front gate. All rice mills in the world are probably brothers when it comes to layout.

Badridas was between thirty-five and forty years of age. He was seated on the mattress he conducted his business from, gathering information about interest rates from the newspapers. When he caught sight of us and learnt our identities, his eyes became uncommonly restless. He darted quick glances into the corners of the room without looking in our direction. His answers to Byomkesh's questions were rather brief and unhelpful. It is not necessary to reproduce the entire interrogation—a few samples are sufficient.

'Did you know Amrito?'

'No.'

'Did you know Sadananda Sur?'

'No.'

'Have you received an anonymous letter?'

'No.'

'Do you own a black horse?'

'No.'

After some more questions and answers Byomkesh prepared to leave. Pinning Badridas down with a searching look, he said, 'I am leaving now, but I shall be back. I shall bring a warrant to search your mill.'

A man of integrity, Badridas did not change his testimony. 'No,' he replied.

We left in exasperation. Barely had we set foot outside the gate when a gaunt individual—a Bengali—accosted us; baring teeth reddened with paan, he said, 'Are you Byomkesh-babu? Were you interrogating Badridas?'

'How did you know?' Byomkesh raised his eyebrows. 'There was no else in there.'

Displaying some more teeth, the man said, 'I was hiding and heard everything. Badridas was lying through his teeth. He knew Amrito, he knew Sadananda Sur, he has received an anonymous letter, he even has a black horse. Such a cunning Marwari, the devil in disguise.'

Sizing the man up, Byomkesh asked calmly, 'Who are you?'

'My name is Rakhal Das. I work for the Marwari.'

'Aren't you afraid of losing your job?'

'I've lost it already. Badridas has given notice, I'll be released at the end of the month.'

'Why has he given notice?'

'Someone from Badridas' community has arrived. He'll get my job. Badridas won't employ Bengalis.'

We began to walk away. The man followed us. 'Don't forget, Byomkesh-babu, that Badridas is as wicked as they come. There's nothing he's not capable of. Counterfeit, fraud, black market . . .'

Without looking back, Byomkesh waved him away.

At the rest house Byomkesh stretched out on the easy chair, looked at the ceiling and said, possibly addressing god, 'The great unknown have you brought to me.'

Taking my shirt off, I sat down by the bed. 'Now that you've met most of them, have you made any sense of it all, Byomkesh?' I asked.

'I've made sense of all of it,' he answered. 'But that is of no use until I identify beyond doubt the man behind all this.'

'What's all this about the black horse? What if Badridas does own a black horse?'

Byomkesh answered, half to himself, 'Something wrong. Badridas' black horse—something wrong.'

'You think the murderer rode a black horse when he went to kill Sadananda Sur? But why? How would it have helped to go on horseback?'

'It would have helped, but it would have done him harm too. So I wonder—never mind.' He cocked his head towards me. 'What did you think of Bishwanath Mallik?'

'He used to be a jockey, loves horses more than dogs; I can't draw at any other conclusions. But was it right to give him all that inside information? What if the news about searching the forest gets out? Won't the criminal be forewarned?'

'Hmm,' answered Byomkesh distractedly. 'But although I have warned him, I believe he will not tell anyone.'

'But what if it slips out!'

'That *is* a cause for concern. Never mind. Nilkantha Adhikari seems a simple soul too. Very loyal to his master, is he not?'

'Yes. But what about Rakhal Das?'

'A skunk. He was out to extract revenge because Badridas sacked him.'

'But was he lying?'

'No, everything he said was true.'

We rested after lunch. Byomkesh looked anxious and worried all the while. I couldn't quite understand the reason for his anxiety.

At four-thirty we left the rest house with the intention of visiting Ramdihi. The train was at a quarter to five, it would reach Ramdihi at ten past five. The chat with Prankeshta Pal would not take long.

We entered the platform after buying our tickets. Checking our tickets at the gate, Monotosh grinned. 'When will you be back?'

'By ten o' clock tonight,' answered Byomkesh.

The passengers were gathered on the platform. The train was due to arrive in about five minutes. Looking around, we discovered the corpulent Inspector Sukhamay conversing furtively with the frail stationmaster Haribilash-babu. Sukhamay-babu waved on spotting us, walking over towards us presently. His eyes were alight with curiosity.

'Going somewhere?'

'To Ramdihi—we have some business there. You?'

'I'm not going anywhere. I'm here to welcome someone. He's coming on this train. Hehe.' His eyebrows danced.

'Who is it?' asked Byomkesh with some surprise.

'His name is Nafar Kundu,' answered Sukhamay-babu. 'When one of the sacks of rice he had dispatched by train burst after a jerk, two kilos of opium were revealed. He's on this train.' He disappeared in the direction of the stationmaster's office, his eyebrows still twitching.

Byomkesh frowned at the square stone tiles on the platform. 'Badridas is here too,' I said.

Byomkesh raised his eyes in a flash. Badridas was approaching from the direction of the warehouse, walking towards us like a crane. It was clear from his behaviour that he had seen us. But he left the platform on slow footsteps without turning his eyes towards us.

Byomkesh's frown deepened.

'Bishu-babu's here too,' I said a minute later. 'What's going on?'

Dressed in jodhpur and breeches, Bishu-babu entered through the gate. On spotting us, he advanced with a smile.

'Hello. Going somewhere?'

'To Ramdihi.'

'Oho—Sadananda Sur's brother-in-law.'

'Yes, we'll be back by ten. And you?'

'I'm expecting a consignment, so I came to enquire about it. Let me check if it's arrived.' Summoning a brief smile to his gaunt face, he went towards the parcel office.

Meanwhile, we could see the steam from the train. The passenger train arrived in a few moments. Before we boarded, we observed a middle-aged man getting off a third-class compartment, surrounded by policemen. I assumed this was the opium-lover Nafar Kundu. He must have gone into hiding out of guilt on receiving the anonymous letter.

The train left after two or three minutes. The doubtful frown on Byomkesh's face was deepening by the second, as though he had suddenly been confronted with a difficult problem and could not make up his mind. 'What's the matter?' I asked. 'You seem to be in a quandary.'

Before he could reply, the train screeched to a halt. Poking my neck through the window, I realized that the train had stopped because it had not received a green signal. The village of Baghmari was visible across the barbed wire.

'This is for the best,' exclaimed Byomkesh, jumping to his feet as though all problems had been solved. 'I am getting off here, Ajit. You had better go on to Ramdihi by yourself. Get everything out of Prankeshta-babu. Don't forget to check whether Sadananda-babu had left his trunk with him or not. All right?'

The train had begun to move slowly after emitting a whistle. Byomkesh jumped off. I looked out the window in bewilderment. Squeezing through the barbed wire, he turned to wave before proceeding towards the village.

9

Byomkesh had never abandoned me like this in the past. The sky seemed to have fallen on my head. How would I interrogate Prankeshta-babu? When Byomkesh conducted his interrogations I enjoyed his technique, but I had never done it myself. Who knew what kind of trouble I'd find myself in? How difficult Byomkesh had made it for me!

The passenger train trundled along; although there was a station every two or three miles along the way, we would soon be at Ramdihi. This was all the time I would have to work things out in my head. The first thing to consider was why Byomkesh wanted to interrogate Prankeshta-babu in the first place. Prankeshta-babu was Sadananda Sur's brother-in-law, and his wife was probably Sadananda-babu's legal heiress, since there was no one else in Sadananda-babu's near family . . . Had Sadananda-babu deposited his trunk with his bother-in-law on his way to Calcutta? Was there anything valuable in the trunk? Prankeshta-babu travelled on this route by trolley in the course of work; it was not at all difficult for him to get off the trolley and go to Baghmari. Did Byomkesh suspect then that Sadananda-babu had been killed by his brother-in-law? . . .

When I reached Ramdihi Junction, it was no trouble at all to get Prankeshta Pal's address. He lived in one of the small cottages surrounded by barbed wire fences near the station. There was a tiny garden in front; a stout man in pantaloons and a sleeveless vest was tending to the garden with a trowel—he stared at me flabbergasted when he caught sight of me.

'Are you Prankeshta Pal?' I asked.

The trowel slipped from his hands. His mouth fell open, and after a few moments he nodded in bewilderment. 'I'm here on behalf of the police,' I told him. 'You must have heard that your brother-in-law Sadananda Sur has died.'

He was so astonished by this that his pantaloons appeared ready to fall off. Jumping in surprise, he disappeared inside the house, calling, 'Sushila! Sushila!'

I was no less astonished. Such behaviour was completely unexpected of someone I had pictured in my mind as the slayer of his wife's brother. He had turned limp at the very mention of the police! Unless . . . all this was just pretence. Hardened criminals resort to all kinds of subterfuge to pull the wool over the eyes of the police—was that what Prankeshta-babu was up to? And who was Sushila? Was she his wife?

Five minutes passed, without any sound emerging from within. Just as I was wondering what to do—hail him, or turn back—Prankeshta-babu became visible near the door. He seemed to have got a grip on himself; his pantaloons were still where they were, but he had donned a bush-shirt over his vest. 'Please come in,' he said, summoning a dying smile to his face.

I entered the drawing room. It was a small room, furnished with inexpensive cane chairs and tables, with a curtained door leading to the rest of the house. The imitation of Western style revealed an attempt at neatness. I sat down with my back to the door leading into the house, while Prankeshta-babu took a seat opposite me.

'So you have been informed of your brother-in-law Sadananda-babu's death,' I began.

'Er . . . yes, yes,' responded Prankeshta-babu, jumping out of his skin.

'When did you learn of the death?'

'Er . . . this morning.'

'Who informed you?'

'Um . . . Haribilash-babu had telephoned from Santalgola.'

'Pardon me, is your wife—Sadananda-babu's sister—here?'

Before he answered, Prankeshta-babu's eyes left my face to dart to the door behind me and return at once.

'Yes, she is.'

I turned my head. The curtain, which was parted slightly, was replaced instantly. It wasn't difficult to realize that Prankeshta-babu's wife Sushila was lurking behind the curtain, directing him from the background.

'Your wife must be devastated.'

Once again Prankeshta-babu darted a glance behind me.

'Yes, absolutely, she is devastated.'

'Your wife is Sadananda-babu's heiress, isn't she?'

'Er . . . no, I don't know. That is to say . . .'

'Where you on cordial terms with Sadananda-babu?'

'Oh yes, extremely cordial.'

'Did you visit each other often?'

'Yes indeed. That is to say . . .'

Once more his eyes darted towards the curtain. 'That is to say . . . not particularly often. Once in a blue moon . . .'

'When did you see him last?'

'Last? Um . . . I can't quite recollect . . .'

'Didn't he visit you at home eleven or twelve days ago?'

'Of course not.' Prankeshta-babu's eyes filled with fear.

'Did he not deposit a steel trunk with you before leaving for Calcutta?'

Prankeshta-babu trembled all over. 'Oh no, a steel trunk . . . But I don't . . .'

'Why are you getting so nervous?' I snapped.

'Nervous! Of course not . . .'

Parting the curtain, Prankeshta-babu's wife entered. Standing behind her husband's chair, she said resolutely, 'My husband is nervous by nature, he becomes even more nervous with strangers. Tell me what you wish to know.'

I took a close look at her. She was about thirty-five, of firm build, with a determined jaw and sharp eyes. Her expression held no sign of grief for her brother. It took me no time at all to realize that she was a formidable woman. I rose to my feet. 'I have learnt all I wished to know, there's nothing more to ask. Goodbye.' I was not up to interrogating Lady Sushila.

Returning to the station, I learnt there was no return train before nine o' clock. To kill the interminable two-and-half hours till then, I drank tea at the shop in the station, smoked my way through numerous cigarettes, and reflected on Prankeshta-babu and his wife.

Prankeshta Pal may have been a nervous sort, but the reason for his excessive anxiety in my presence was not just because of the state of his nerves. There must have been other reasons too. What were they? Prankeshta-babu had told me several lies on his wife's instructions. For instance? For instance, whether or not Sadananda Sur was on cordial terms with Pranakeshta-babu, he did frequent his brother-in-law's home. He had deposited his steel trunk with his brother-in-law before leaving for Calcutta eleven or twelve days ago. There must have been something valuable in the trunk. What could it have been? Was it money? Jewellery? Weapons? It was difficult to hazard a guess. But Lady Sushila may not have succeeded in containing her curiosity about the contents of the trunk and may have broken the lock. Nothing was impossible for a woman as formidable as she was. But after that? Maybe what they had discovered in the trunk had made it imperative to kill Sadananda Sur. Maybe the trunk contained a hand grenade, which had been used to . . .

But no. However indomitable a woman Lady Sushila might be, would she really murder her own brother? And it was completely impossible for Pranakeshta Pal to have been involved in such an audacious crime . . . But why had Haribilash-babu the stationmaster been in such a hurry to pass on the bad news to his friend? Was it comradely empathy? . . .

I returned to Santalgola at nine o' clock. The moon was up, the town and marketplace were hushed. I had expected to find Byomkesh back at the rest house. But he was nowhere to be seen. Where was he?

His cooking done, the servant at the rest house was nodding off on the veranda. I told him to serve the food, cover it, and go home. He left.

Dimming the lamp, I stretched myself out on the bed. The moonlight filtered in through the window at the back . . . Where had Byomkesh disappeared? He had got off the train all of a sudden. What had he been up to in Baghmari all this time?

I had dropped off; I awoke to the sound of Byomkesh whispering in my ear, 'Wake up, Ajit, come and see this.'

'What . . . ?' I said, sitting up with a start.

'Shh! Quietly now!' Taking my arm, Byomkesh led me off the bed towards the window at the back; pointing outside, he asked, 'Can you see them?'

I hadn't rubbed the sleep out of my eyes yet;Byomkesh's behaviour had made me expect an extraordinary sight. But I could only stare at what I saw. In a clearing amidst weeds and bushes about fifteen or twenty feet away sat six or seven dark-coloured beasts in a semicircle, looking up at the moon. At first sight they had appeared to be black dogs. 'Black dogs,' I said. But when they cried out in unison the very next moment, my doubts were dispelled. A group of jackals was having its own musical soiree under the moonlight.

Byomkesh burst into laughter at the expression on my face. Startled, the jackals loped off. 'What's all this?' I asked. 'What's the point of waking me up to stare at jackals in the middle of the night?'

'Have you ever seen jackals by moonlight?' asked Byomkesh.

'What happens when you see jackals by moonlight?'

'You are blessed, the darkness of ignorance is dispelled. Now let us eat, I'm famished.'

Turning the lamp up, we sat down to our dinner. I noticed that although Byomkesh was dispatching the food to his mouth like a starving man, he looked cheerful. 'What are you looking so happy about?' I enquired. 'Where were you out so late? Were you in Baghmari?'

'I was done at Baghmari by nine o' clock,' he replied. 'After that . . .'

'What business did you have at Baghmari?'

'I had to meet Patal, Dashu and Gopal.'

'I see, you won't tell me. Very well then, and after that?'

'Then I returned to Santalgola and paid Inspector Sukhamay a visit. That took an hour. Then I went to the station. Haribilash-babu was not there; he had to be roused from his bed. I had to make a long phone call. There are no more than five people at the police station here, ten more will arrive in the morning. I returned only after I had made all the arrangements.'

'So you don't need to know what Prankeshta-babu said?' I asked.

'Of course I do. Tell me all.'

I described everything down to the last detail. Byomkesh listened closely, but displayed no interest. Washing his hands after the meal, he said, 'In every couple, if one is an idiot, the other is vicious. This is the rule of nature.'

After we sat down, I asked, 'What's that in your pocket?'

Byomkesh was a little startled, even a little embarrassed. 'A gun . . . meaning, a pistol,' he said.

'Where did you get it?'

'At the police station. This is Inspector Sukhamay's pistol.'

'Hmm. I see you don't want to give explanations. Let's go to bed then.'

'You go to bed, I have to be awake all night. What if the person with the hand grenade is afraid? It's best to be careful.'

'Then I shall stay up too.'

We passed the night in wakefulness. Fortunately there were no disturbances. Over a cup of tea in the early hours of the morning, Byomkesh's tongue finally loosened, and I learnt the identity of our unknown bird.

10

We went out at seven in the morning. Byomkesh wrapped a shawl around himself to ensure that his pistol did not attract attention.

There was no flurry of activity in the shops or on the road yet. Only a bullock cart or two, along with a horse-drawn carriage here and there, were moving about. We entered Badridas the Marwari's mill.

He was sitting on his haunches outside his house, brushing his teeth, a jar of water by his side. He did not notice us at first, but when we came closer, his eyes began to roll like a trapped bird fluttering its wings desperately in a cage; his rustic toothbrush made of a twig slipped from his fingers.

'You'll have to come with us, Sethji,' said Byomkesh.

'Wha . . . at!' asked Badridas, half-rising from his position before falling back.

'We're going to conduct a search,' explained Byomkesh. 'As an eminent citizen hereabouts, we want you as a witness.'

'Oh no . . . ' he protested, taking the jar of water and retreating rapidly towards a specific destination.

We left again. It took about five minutes to reach Bishwanath Mallik's mill.

We met chief accountant Nilkantha Adhikari near the gate. 'So early?' he enquired, deferentially touching his forehead with joined palms.

'Where's your master?' queried Byomkesh.

'In his room, having a cup of tea.'

'Come, let us pay him a visit.'

'Very well.'

Biswanath Mallik was seated at the table in his room, breakfasting on bread and butter and a half-boiled egg; his jaws ceased their mastication at our sight. An unnatural noise emerged from his throat: 'Byomkesh-babu!'

'We had no choice but to be here early in the morning,' Byomkesh informed him. 'But there is no hurry, do finish your meal.'

'What do you want?' slurred Bishu-babu, pushing his egg away. His gaunt face was slowly losing colour.

'I had concluded yesterday that it would be pointless to search your mill,' Byomkesh answered. 'But today I feel otherwise.'

The veins on Bishu-babu's temple began to throb—he appeared on the verge of exploding. But he restrained himself with supreme effort, and an expression resembling a smile appeared on his lips. 'Why did you change your mind suddenly?' he asked.

'I have my reasons,' responded Byomkesh. 'I did not go to Ramdihi last evening, I was hidden near the cotton tree in that forest of yours. Three of the village lads were with me. What we saw last night has compelled me to change my mind, Bishwanath-babu.'

Bishwanatah-babu's eyes flared for an instant. Lighting a cigarette with a shaking hand, he lazily extracted a key-ring from his breast-pocket and twirled it around his finger, asking, 'And what if I do not allow my mill to be searched?'

'Your willingness is irrelevant,' said Byomkesh. 'I have a search warrant.'

'Let me see your warrant.'

As Byomkesh put his hand in his pocket, Bishu-babu attempted to unlock his drawer in a flash with the key.

When Byomkesh brought his hand out of his pocket, it held a pistol. 'Do not open the drawer,' he said.

Bishu Mallik turned his head like a cornered wild cat; at the sight of the pistol in Byomkesh's hand he abandoned his attempt to open the drawer, but a threatening hiss emerged from his throat.

'Blow the whistle, Ajit,' ordered Byomkesh.

I was prepared with the police whistle in my pocket—I blew it loudly.

Within a minute the room filled with Inspector Sukhamay Samanta and his followers. 'Arrest Bishwanath Mallik and handcuff him, Inspector Samanta,' instructed Byomkesh. 'He has the key to the drawer, open it. Be careful, the weapons are in there.'

Bishwanath Mallik could not be arrested easily—he bit and scratched like a wild cat. It took five or six people to overcome him eventually and clamp the handcuffs on his wrists. When the drawer was opened, it revealed twenty-six .38 automatics, innumerable cartridges and fourteen hand grenades. They were worth at least twenty thousand rupees in the black market.

Surrounded by the police, Bishwanath Mallik pulsed with impotent rage. Suddenly he said aggressively, 'All right, I deal in stolen arms. But is there any proof that I murdered Amrito and Sadananda Sur?'

'The court will decide whether there is,' answered Byomkesh calmly. 'One of these pistols is the one with which you killed Amrito. The bullet was found in Amrito's body.

It will not be difficult to prove in a ballistic examination.'

Bishwanath Mallik's eyes glazed over, striking himself on the forehead with his handcuffs, he collapsed.

11

At three that afternoon, we were stretched out on two beds in the rest house after lunch. Patal, Dashu and Gopal had departed after repeated acts of homage to Byomkesh's skills. Having dispatched the accused to headquarters, Inspector Sukhamay Samanta was trying to prove to the other policemen at the police station over a heaped plate of egg fritters that his part in the apprehension of the suspected murderer was not insignificant. After a brief lull in activities, the town was back to its usual bustle: one for one and two for two. A pair of unknowns named Amrito and Sadananda Sur may have faced untimely deaths, but the regular flow of life had not been interrupted. It would not be, either, even if their assailant were to hang at the gallows. One for one and two for two . . . rest in piece, both of you . . .

Looking at the ceiling, Byomkesh sighed; 'I have no regrets over Sadananda Sur's death,' he said, 'but young Amrito died quite unnecessarily.'

'Tell me the whole story from the beginning,' I said.

'This story begins with Sadananda Sur,' said Byomkesh. 'Had it not been for him, we would not have succeeded in apprehending the illegal arms dealer. We can start with him.

'From what I have understood of Sadananda Sur's nature, he was parsimonious and reticent. He did not enjoy revealing his secrets. His finances were indifferent. He had paid for his sister's wedding, but had never married himself. An ancestral house and a little land; a little trading in rice at Santalgola; a little money from selling Ayurvedic medicine—these were his sources of income. Since he lived alone, he eked out a living somehow.

'But he was not free of earthly desires. It is true that the parsimonious never like spending their own money to fulfil their wants, but no one can claim they haven't any. Sadananda-babu had the craving, but not the cash. Perhaps he saved a few pennies from his small income, but his nature didn't allow him to spend them on pleasure for himself. The days went by this way. He was getting older; his capacity for enjoyment was shrinking as well. Perhaps he would have spent all his life unfulfilled this way. But suddenly, at the age of forty-five, a big opportunity presented itself.

'Sadananada-babu used to frequent Bishwanaath-babu's mill. The vials of Ayurvedic medicine found in Bishwanath Mallik's safe must have been supplied by Sadananda-babu. This was the route to their intimacy. Then Sadananda-babu unexpectedly got to know the deepest secret of Bishu Mallik's life—his business of dealing in illegal arms. It is hard to say how he came to know, perhaps he had found out where Bishu Mallik kept the weapons hidden. The cotton tree was not very far from Sadananda-babu's home; maybe he had spotted Bishu Mallik there.

'Sadananda-babu could have stolen the weapons and bombs, but that was not the path he took. Sadananda-babu was not experienced enough to be aware of how to sell weapons in the black market. He adopted a different route. I want money, or I'll expose you, he told Bishu Mallik. Simple blackmail, in other words.

'Bishu Mallik was helpless. He had to part with five hundred rupees. Sadananda-babu went home with this money. His time for pleasure was running out, he could delay no longer. He decided to visit Calcutta.

'But he was circumspect by nature, not in favour of taking all the money with himself. However, leaving it in his empty house meant risking theft. So he decided on a different course of action.

'Much of what I am telling you is conjecture, but not wild imagination. Sadananda-babu put most of the money he had got in a steel trunk, added whatever he had saved, perhaps even some jewellery of old that he might have inherited. Then he left, the steel trunk in one hand and a canvas bag for his own use in the other. He had planned to deposit the trunk with his sister and brother-in-law at Ramdihi, and then go on his pleasure trip to Calcutta.

'Sadananda Sur went on his way, but meanwhile Bishu Mallik was in a spot. He had been running his business without trouble all this time, but now he was trapped. As long as Sadananda Sur was alive, there was no deliverance for him, for Sadananda would continue his extortion. He decided to get rid of Sadananda Sur; he was intelligent, and he was in possession of lethal weapons. Getting rid of Sadananda would not prove difficult.

'Having deposited his trunk at his sister's house, Sadananda was probably having a good time in Calcutta when Bishu Mallik rode into the forest on his horse after sunset one evening and took a grenade from his cache in the cotton tree to booby-trap Sadananda's house. As soon as Sadananda tried to enter his house on his return from Calcutta, the grenade would explode.

'But some other things happened before Sadananda returned. Whenever Bishu Mallik needed to sell some weapons, he would ride into the forest. Around ten o'clock one night, Amrito spotted the horse while looking for his calf. He mistook it for the ghost of a horse. When he re-entered the forest on the instigation of his friends, he discovered not just the horse but also its rider under the cotton tree.

'Bishu Mallik was probably on his way back that night after having booby-trapped Sadananda Sur's house. They knew each other; Amrito had applied to Bishu Mallik for a job. Bishu Mallik realized that when the booby trap exploded, Amrito would testify to having seen Bishu Mallik behind Sadananda Sur's house that night. Amrito may even have spotted him when he was jumping over the wall at the back of Sadananda's house. Therefore it was not safe to let Amrito live. Bishu Mallik had an automatic pistol; murdering Amrito, he disappeared on horseback.

'When I investigated the scene of the crime, what I found strangest was the horse. Amrito had seen a ghost horse, but what I saw were the hoof prints of a living beast. A horse was connected with this case. We still did not know who the criminal was, but whoever he might be, he came into the forest on horseback. Why?

'Travelling on horseback was quick, but it attracted attention. A person intent on committing a crime does not want to attract attention; why then did this person enter the forest on horseback? There must be a reason. What reason? Was it to jump over Sadananda Sur's high back wall? It was easier to jump over a wall off a horse's back, and there was a guava tree on the other side to help the descent. But was that all? Or was there more to it? I received the answer last night. But more of that later.

'Sadananda Sur returned home as planned. He had not brought the trunk back—perhaps he had intended to visit his brother-in-law after a couple of days' rest to fetch the trunk. But this wish was not fulfilled. He died practically before our eyes while trying to enter his own home.

'After his death, it all became clear to me. The person I was here to apprehend had murdered both Amrito and Sadananda Sur. Those who had bought the weapons were outsiders, but the murderer was not an outsider; both Amrito and Sadananda Sur knew him. Amrito had spotted him and Sadananda Sur had started extorting money from him. Only two things remained unknown—who was he? And why did he ride into the forest on a black horse?

'Amrito had said the black ghost horse had flames coming out of its nostrils. It may have all been his fevered imagination. On the other hand, it could have been partly true. Therefore it became necessary to investigate the black horse.

'Enquiries revealed that there was just one black horse in Santalgola, which belonged to Badridas the Marwari. Was Badridas the culprit then? He is as slippery as an eel; he is capable of selling adulterated rice, his parochialism can be extreme; but he lacks the courage to kill even one, let alone two, persons. Besides, to picture him riding a horse is utterly impossible.

'One outcome of my anonymous letter was that some people could be removed from the list of suspects. Jamnadas Gangaram showed the letter to the police, so it was not him. I had suspected Nafar Kundu at first, but he turned out not to own a horse. No one would borrow a horse for a murder. I eliminated Prankeshta Pal from the list at the outset. It was possible to take a trolley to Baghmari, but since porters would also be travelling on the trolley, it wouldn't be easy to commit a murder without their knowledge. I was only curious to know what Sadananda Sur's trunk held.

'At any rate, the list of suspects was pruned to just three—Badridas the Marwari, Bishu Mallik and Inspector Sukhamay. I could not eliminate the inspector, for he does possess a horse, though it is not black. And no one would find it easier to run a business of this kind. It is always darkest under the lamp.

'But when I learnt that Bishu Mallik had been a jockey once, all my suspicion centred on him. I came to know, moreover, that he had lent Sadananda Sur five hundred rupees. It was in fact not a loan but a bribe. No businessman would lend money without conditions to someone as insolvent as Sadananda Sur.

'I set a trap for Bishu Mallik, revealing everything on my mind and in my heart to him. I had always thought it possible to keep the weapons hidden in the forest. I had assumed they were buried somewhere in the ground near the cotton tree. When Bishu Mallik heard we were planning to search the forest, he began to worry. It was true that the weapons were concealed very carefully indeed, but you never knew, the police might still unearth them. Bishu Mallik would not be caught, but weapons worth a lot of money would be confiscated. Bishu Mallik was overcome by greed.

'When I was taking the train for Ramdihi last evening, Bishu Mallik turned up to make sure I was indeed going. I had in fact not planned to go all the way to Ramdihi; I had decided to get off at the next station and return to Baghmari. But fate was on my side, for the train stopped next to the village.

'In the village I got hold of Patal, Dashu and Gopal and went into the forest with them. It was impossible to search the entire forest, but I scoured the area between the back wall of Sadananda Sur's house—where the hoof print had been found—and the roots of the cotton tree for signs of freshly-dug earth. But I discovered nothing.

'What next? Sunset was not far away. I planned my next move over a cigarette. Let us go to Santalgola, I told the boys.

'We walked through the forest to reach the edge of Santalgola. The forest was nearly a hundred and fifty yards wide here; the station was at one side, the cooperative bank on the other, and Bishu Mallik's mill, halfway between them. This was the back of the mill, with a small gate set in the barbed wire fence. I explained my plan to Patal. They would climb into trees spaced evenly apart at the edge of the forest and hide themselves, keeping their eyes peeled for anyone entering the forest on horseback or on foot. They would try to identify him, but in no circumstances must they try to apprehend him.

'Patal climbed a tree directly opposite Bishu Mallik's mill, Dashu went off towards the station and Gopal, towards the bank. There was a moon in the sky that evening too; even at night no one would be able to enter the forest without their noticing.

'Once they had settled into their trees, I went back towards the cotton tree. This tree had planted many a doubt in my mind. Amrito was killed beneath it. If the key to this mystery lay anywhere near the forest, it had to be somewhere near the tree.

'When I returned to the tree the sun had set and the moon had risen. I climbed into a shaggy treetop some twenty or twenty-five yards away. I planned to wait there like a tiger hunter. I had no weapon, I was here only to observe Mr Tiger. I did not know if he would come at all, but if he did, it would certainly be before nine.

'The cotton had shed most of its leaves, so that there was

no shade beneath the tree. The higher the moon rose, the brighter the light became. Suddenly a cuckoo called out from a nearby tree. What a strange situation. There I was, waiting for a glimpse of a vicious murderer, and here was a cuckoo! How strange the world is!

'Quite some time passed. Peering at my watch, I saw it was a quarter to eight. At once I heard the sound of footsteps crunching on dry leaves. Turning my head, I saw a horse emerging from the shadows at a stately pace. A black horse. On its back sat a man dressed in black. I could not see his face, but he was crouched like a jockey, casting wary glances around him.

'The horse made straight for the trunk of the cotton and stopped close to it, as still as a statue. What I witnessed thereafter was a circus act. The horseman sprang to his feet, standing on the horse. Then he reached into a hole in the trunk. There was an opening like a cubbyhole about ten feet from the ground, where the foliage began. A nest for some unknown bird.

'Now do you see why the culprit visited the forest on horseback? The weapons were not buried in the ground; they were in the cubbyhole ten feet from it. The cotton trunk is covered with thick scaly thorns; people don't climb this tree, not even squirrels. No other hiding place could be so safe. Of course, you could use a ladder to climb it, but who was going to set a ladder there? And carrying a ladder into the forest would attract attention. A horse was far safer, especially if it happened to have been trained by a jockey.

'Anyway, the rider had a bag in his left hand. Reaching into the hole with his right hand, he transferred the weapons to the bag one by one. By then I had recognized the rider—it was Bishu Mallik. Even without seeing his face, there was no mistaking the short, slim figure and the bow legs. My surmise was correct. But one more puzzle remained: where had Mallik acquired a black horse? He was far too clever to have lied to me if he indeed possessed one. As a matter of fact, he had not understood the significance of my question when I had asked him about the black horse. He had not even imagined that a black horse had anything to do with this case. I unravelled the mystery of the black horse at the dead of night, after returning home.

'More of that later. Meanwhile, Bishu Mallik resumed his seat on the horse, his bag now full, and cantered back. I dismounted from the tree after he had disappeared into the shadows. The watch showed the time as a quarter past eight. I set off towards the spot where Patal and the others were hiding. My plan had worked out; since the police were to search the forest the next day, Bishu Mallik had removed the weapons the night before. The question now was: where would he stash them? It was not enough to nab the criminal; we had to get the arms too. In fact, apprehending the person without finding the weapons would be useless.

'When I reached the edge of the forest, Patal and the others had not yet dismounted; they did so on seeing me. All three were excited; they had spotted the rider entering the forest and recognized him. Bishu Mallik had emerged from the back gate of his rice mill on horseback, riding practically past Patal's tree into the forest. He had returned after forty minutes, riding back into the mill through the same gate.

'I asked: are you quite sure he went back through his own gate and not anywhere else?

'No, answered Patal, he didn't go anywhere else.

'I was relieved. Bishu Mallik would keep the weapons in the mill, at least until the police had completed its search of the forest. I had told him in the morning that we would not search the mill, which he had believed. Bishu Mallik must have considered me a rather simple soul.

'Clapping the boys on their backs, I told them: I have solved Amrito's murder thanks to you. But do not ask any more questions tonight, come back tomorrow at nine in the morning, you will get to know everything. But remember, not a word to anyone.

'They went back to the village, and I, to the police station. Collecting a pistol from Inspector Sukhamay I went to the railway station. When I returned after making all the arrangements it was the middle of the night and you were snoring your head off.

'Without waking you, I went up to the window at the back. I saw some animals outside. At first I thought they were black dogs, but then I realized they were jackals, not dogs. At once the mystery of the black dog became clear. Jackals are not black, they are brown. Yet they appeared black. The horse was not black either, it was dark brown;

chestnut, as they say. All dark shades appear black from a distance in the moonlight. That was why Amrito had seen a black ghost horse, and I had seen a black horse too. This is the mystery of the black horse. I have no objection to calling it the joke of the black horse either.

'At the dinner table you recounted the story of Prankeshta Pal and his wife. It is not difficult to see where they went wrong. Prankeshta Pal was competent at his work, but his writ did not run large in his own home, where his wife ruled. Sadananda-babu had indeed left his trunk with his sister. It had not been broken open at first; but when his sister Sushila learnt of his death, she did not hesitate any more. She broke the lock open and seized whatever she found. Maybe she will eventually inherit her brother's assets anyway, but you can never tell with the law. It is wise to grab what is at hand. This was sister Sushila's psychology. But Prankeshta Pal is a man who knows right from wrong, which is why he became nervous in your presence . . .

'And then? There is nothing more to tell. Now it is time for Vedvyas to rest. Who knows how many more great men like Bishu Mallik are meditating in silence in the wonder that is India!'

With a gigantic yawn, Byomkesh turned on his side. 'It is almost dawn,' he said. 'Get some sleep while you can, we are returning to Calcutta tonight. Hehe.'

Translator's Note

He's not like your dad, or even your granddad. He'd be older than either of them now, though he might still be a detective. Or, as he liked to call himself, a seeker of truth. Because, to Byomkesh Bakshi, gentleman detective, the truth was not about discovering who had committed the crime. It was about finding out who the evil person was and ensuring that they were punished. No wonder the police didn't like him much. Not only did Byomkesh show them up as bumbling idiots time and again, he even let murderers go free sometimes if he felt that the murdered person had been the real villain of the piece.

Translating these Byomkesh Bakshi stories, then, is like translating them thrice over. The first translation is straightforward: telling the story in English instead of Bengali. Which means transferring the storyteller's descriptions, analysis and confusion—the stories are told by Byomkesh's dim (compared to him, anyhow) sidekick Ajit—from Bengali to English. But wait a minute, it's not that simple. Because the Bengali used in the original was a very formal, often ornate, sort of language, with long sentences and the use of what was called *shadhu bhasha*—or a classical form of Bengali which was used only in books and not how people actually spoke.

Don't forget, this is the period between the 1930s and the 1950s we're talking about. Roughly when your grandparents were growing up, and your parents probably weren't born. So, they used a slightly bizarre—by today's standards, that is—form of the language when they wrote their books. (They spoke just the same as other people, though.) That's the second translation then, across something like seventy years, give or take ten. If Byomkesh and Ajit decided to speak in English back then, it might not have been exactly how they sound here in these stories. We modernized things just a little bit.

That's not all. Because of the distance caused by the years and by the geography, you might have found some references in the stories quite impossible to understand. We've converted all of them to expressions and relationships that make sense today. Just about the only things left unchanged are some of the ways in which people addressed each other formally—such as adding a 'babu' at the end of someone's name, for instance. Don't be misled by the formality, though—Byomkesh continued to use the word, perhaps in mock respect, even after he knew who the murderer was.

So, what's the third translation? It's not in the words you read, it's in your head. When you read these stories, you mustn't think of Byomkesh and Ajit—or the criminals they're chasing—living next door. Because Calcutta—and every other place in the country, for that matter—looked very different then. If at all possible, check the family album for photographs going back to the 1950s, or even earlier, to see what the city was like, how the streets appeared, what kind of clothes people wore. Or, just get on to the Net and surf along to http://bit.ly/oldcalcutta. You'll find some interesting photographs. And you'll know why you have to translate the pictures in your head from your present to the time your grandparents were about your age.

Oh yes, a lot has changed from the time these stories were written. But what hasn't is the nature of crime. Just like they do now, back then, too, twisted people had no compunctions stealing, robbing, and even killing if necessary to feed their own greed. Hence, if Byomkesh Bakshi were to get into a time travel machine and visit us here and now, he'd find that while a lot of other things have changed, crime and criminals haven't. And he'd be solving mysteries with the same brilliance today.

That's why we translated these stories for you. And here's our suggestion: after you've read them, read them out to your parents. Even your grandparents, if you like. Because nothing reduces the generation gap than cracking a good detective story. Or three. As Byomkesh might have said, 'Let's go.'

2012 Arunava Sinha

Arunava Sinha is a translator of classic and contemporary Bengali fiction. His translation of Sankar's Chowringhee *won the Vodafone-Crossword translation prize in 2007, and was shortlisted for the Independent Best Foreign Fiction prize in the UK in the year 2009.*

Fourteen of his translations from Bengali into English have been published so far. He was born and educated in Calcutta, and now lives in New Delhi with his wife and son.

PUFFIN CLASSICS

The Rhythm of Riddles

Three Byomkesh Bakshi Mysteries

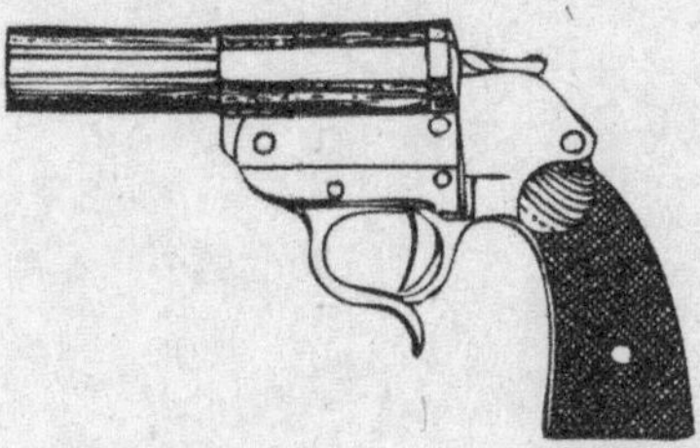

With Puffin Classics, the story isn't over
when you reach the final page.
Want to discover more about the author
and his world?
Read on . . .

CONTENTS

AUTHOR FILE

NAME: Saradindu Bandyopadhyay
BORN: 30 March 1899 in Jaunpur, Uttar Pradesh.
EDUCATION: Graduated from Vidyasagar College, Calcutta. Studied law in Patna.
LITERARY CAREER:
Known in Bengal for his detective novels, a large number of short stories on a variety of topics, historical novels and even children's literature.

Published his first book—a collection of poems—called *Jouban Smriti* (Memories of Youth) while he was still in college. Started writing short stories while studying and practising law in Patna. Published his first Byomkesh novella in 1932—and the character remained hugely popular till his death. (He had an unfinished Byomkesh story at the time of his death.)

Moved to Bombay in 1938 and became a screenplay writer for Bombay Talkies, which was the leading film production house of that time. Stayed and worked in Bombay for nearly fifteen years. Continued to write in Bengali after his return to Calcutta and became one of the most popular authors of his time.
ON-SCREEN ADAPTATIONS:
Many of the Byomkesh stories have been made into films.

Satyajit Ray made one of his stories, 'Chiriakhana' (The Zoo), into a Bengali film starring the biggest star of the times, Uttam Kumar, as the detective.

The adaptation that made the detective a household name all over India was a television series—*Byomkesh Bakshi*—made for Doordarshan, starring Rajit Kapur in the title role. It was made in the early 1990s, had a very successful run and is still seen on re-runs.
DIED: 22 September, 1970

FIVE FACTS ABOUT BYOMKESH

1. Every detective has a distinctive style of solving cases. Actually, even when they aren't solving cases, they usually impress their clients and sidekicks with smart inferences drawn from observing things closely. Byomkesh's pet trick was to predict the look and manner of a person by the way he knocked on the door.
2. Byomkesh did not like the terms 'detective' or 'investigator'. He called himself a Satyanweshi. Derived from the Sanskrit words 'satya' and 'anweshi', it literally means 'seeker of truth'.
3. Byomkesh fell in love and married a lady called Satyabati. He hinted about this to his friend-cum-foil Ajit by saying that he is always seeking 'satya'!
4. In the stories, Byomkesh did not wear glasses but in Satyajit Ray's film, he had glasses. Subsequently, most film and TV adaptations have Byomkesh wearing glasses. In an interview, Saradindu expressed his displeasure at his hero wearing glasses in the film.
5. Byomkesh's father was a teacher of Mathematics and he himself holds a Physics degree—which explains his analytical bent of mind. It was Ajit who taught him to play chess, but within a few days, Byomkesh became better than his teacher and would outdo him at every game!

SARADINDU'S CONTRIBUTION TO CHILDREN'S LITERATURE

Apart from Byomkesh, he created another popular character—Sadashiv—for children.

This young boy was an orphan, growing up in rural Maharashtra during the times when Chhatrapati Shivaji was fighting the Mughals and Bijapur royals to establish an independent Maratha kingdom.

Saradindu wrote a series of stories covering the teen years of Sadashiv's life, when he runs away from home and joins Shivaji's army. In every story, Sadashiv managed to help the Maratha king by taking on a secret mission and destroying the enemy's plan with his bravery and intelligence.

Apart from Sadashiv and Shivaji, the stories had very authentic depictions of other historic characters like Jijabai (Shivaji's mother) and Tanaji (Shivaji's childhood friend and one of his generals).

There are five novellas of Sadashiv's adventures (published between 1958 and 1962). Saradindu's notebooks revealed notes and drafts of four more episodes. He wanted to trace Shivaji's entire life through the eyes of Sadashiv, but unfortunately he passed away before the completion of these books.

Sadashiv's adventures are available in a book called Band of Soldiers: A Year on the Road with Shivaji *by Saradindu Bandyopadhyay; translated by Sreejata Guha. Puffin Books.*

THINGS TO THINK ABOUT

Partition of India

In the first story 'Rhythm of Riddles', one of the characters suffered a major loss during the Partition of India.

The Partition of India happened in 1947, when India was divided into three parts at the time of its independence from British rule. This division was based on religious strife. Hence Hindu-dominated areas formed India while the Muslim-dominated areas in the East formed East Pakistan (which later became Bangladesh), and those in the West formed Pakistan.

The states of Punjab and Bengal were divided between the two countries. Since the division was made on religious grounds, it is estimated that more than 7 million people migrated from India to Pakistan and nearly an equal number moved from Pakistan to India.

Both the governments were newly formed and were unable to handle such massive transfers of population as well as the religious tensions. As a result, there were widespread riots between the Hindus and Muslims leading to large-scale loss of life and property.

Do you know of any other books and movies which are based on the Partition of India? Do you have any members of your family (perhaps, your grandparents) who were there when the Partition happened?

Seeing Ghosts

In the second story 'The Death of Amrito' as well as the third 'Byomkesh and Barada', there are descriptions of ghost sightings.

Ghosts are spirits of dead people that become 'visible' to the living. According to most theories, when a person has an unnatural death, his spirit (or soul) refuses to leave the living world due to its 'unfulfilled desires'.

For many centuries, there have been reports of people 'seeing ghosts' but they have usually been negated by rationalists as hallucinations or any unusual physical characteristics of the 'haunted location'.

In films as well as books, ghosts are shown in different forms. Can you name some films or books that show ghosts in the following forms?

Invisible—not seen by anybody but voice can be heard	
Invisible—can be seen or heard by one (or a few)	
Barely visible, smoky shapes	
Regular, human-like shapes (indistinguishable from living human beings)	

Can you think of any other form in which a ghost has appeared in a book you have read or a film you have seen?

Do you know anybody—friends or family—who has seen a ghost? Ask him to describe the whole incident in detail and try to see if there is any logical explanation to the 'ghost's' appearance.

Calling Ghosts

'Ghost hobbyists' often try to call the spirits of departed souls for a conversation. One of the common techniques used for this uncommon pastime is planchette (as described in 'Byomkesh and Barada').

Planchette is usually done through a 'medium'—a person through whom the ghost communicates. Often, the communication is done by the medium holding a pencil above a paper and the ghost writing through him. Quite obviously, a medium can write on his own and there is a high chance of deception.

Another method is to keep a pointer on a board with letters and numbers printed on it. As the ghost appears, the pointer moves from letter to letter spelling out answers to the questions posed to him.

Would you like to call ghosts? Whose ghost would you call? And what questions would you ask him (or her)?

Name of the Detective

Saradindu Bandyopadhyay once said in an interview that for a character to be memorable, it must have a catchy name.

Byomkesh Bakshi is certainly one of the catchiest names in detective fiction—both the name and surname being uncommon but not rare in isolation. In its combined form, the name becomes alliterative and unique. In one of his stories, Byomkesh said that the British professors of his college pronounced his name as Bomb Case!

Let us take a look at the names of the most famous detectives in fiction and see how catchy they are.

Sherlock Holmes	The most famous detective in history has a very unusual name, which literally means 'fair haired'. Sherlock's elder brother also had a very unusual name—Mycroft.
Hercule Poirot	Both the name and the surname of Agatha Christie's detective are quite uncommon. The first name is the French version of the Greek hero, Hercules. The detective took his name quite seriously and towards the end of his career, he undertook twelve tasks that were quite similar to the Greek hero's.
Father Brown	G.K. Chesterton's famous detective—who was a Catholic priest—on the other hand, had a very common name. Even his first name is not clear from the stories and he remains a bit of a mystery.

Victoria Iphigenia Warshawski	Usually known as V.I. Warshawski, this is a lady private investigator working in Chicago.
Sam Spade	Again, an alliterative name made up of a very common first name and surname. Created by Dashiell Hammett, he was the hero of stories like *The Maltese Falcon* that were also made into hugely popular films.
Prodosh C. Mitter a.k.a. Feluda	Satyajit Ray's famous detective takes a set of relatively common names to create a name which eventually became iconic. And his pet name was common to the point of being almost silly!

There are many more: Nancy Drew, Miss Marple et al. Would you like to list out a few?

Read More in Puffin Classics

The Burmese Box: Two Novellas

Lila Majumdar

Translated from the Bengali by Srilata Banerjee

'I'm going to find that box, the box that's been missing for a hundred years . . . Do you know, there are precious gems in it, worth a king's ransom? Emeralds the size of a rooster's egg, rubies as big as pigeons' eggs, pearls the size of a duck's egg!'

Aunt Podi's treasured Burmese box was a part of family history. When Panchu Mama narrates the hair-raising story of how it was acquired and the mysterious circumstances in which it got lost, Goopy decides to find the fabled box and its precious contents.

'The Burmese Box' is an action-packed story of a family on a treasure hunt, as they grapple with devious plans and nasty crooks, a highly suspicious detective and eccentric relatives.

In 'Goopy's Secret Diary', con men, hidden treasures, a stolen necklace and the secret of an old mansion make for a fascinating read as we follow Goopy's rollicking adventures in a forest.

Featuring two novellas, *The Burmese Box* is beloved children's author Lila Majumdar at her best. Her impeccable style and trademark humour will keep generations of readers in thrall.

Read More in Puffin Classics

One Dozen Stories

Satyajit Ray

Translated from the Bengali by Gopa Majumdar

Twelve timeless stories by a master storyteller.

The creator of immortal films, Satyajit Ray was also a writer of great repute. In this collection are some of his most extraordinary and gripping stories that will take readers to realms of adventure, fantasy and horror. While 'Bonku Babu's Friend' deals with a mofussil schoolteacher's encounter with a friendly and somewhat awkward alien, 'Anath Babu's Terror' is the tale of a ghost hunter's foray into a haunted house. Meet Bipin Chowdhury, who seems to be suffering from a most disagreeable bout of amnesia, and read the amazing story of a carnivorous plant with a monstrous appetite in 'The Hungry Septopus'. This collection also includes two stories featuring everyone's favourite detective, Feluda.

Published originally in Bengali as *Ek Dojon Goppo*, this collection—the first in a series of short stories written by the master storyteller—is funny, sinister and intriguing by turns and truly a must-have.

Chandrakanta

Devakinandan Khatri

Translated from the Hindi and retold by Deepa Agarwal

Chandrakanta's eyes grew wide when she discovered a huge stone crane right in the middle of the ruins. The moment she drew closer, the bird opened its mouth. Alarmed, Chandrakanta moved away, and accidentally stepped on a stone slab. Immediately, the crane swung around, opened its beak and swallowed Chandrakanta!

The dashing Prince Virendra of Naugarh is madly in love with the breathtakingly beautiful Princess Chandrakanta of Vijaygarh. But there are obstacles galore in the paths of the lovers. There are evil ministers with sinister magicians at their beck and call, enemy kings only too happy to go into battle, masters of disguise who can fool the cleverest of spies, and magic all around. Then Chandrakanta gets trapped in a fantastic maze, from which only Virendra can rescue her. But will he be able to decipher the clues, follow the trail correctly and get to her before it is too late? And will their friends, Tej Singh, Chapla and the others, help them adequately with their deep knowledge of the art of divination and disguise?

A rollicking story of fantasy and adventure, *Chandrakanta* has been read and loved since 1888, when the book was published serially in short chapters. The first mystery novel in Hindi, and the biggest popular bestseller of its age, *Chandrakanta* was a trailblazer. This modern translation and retelling of a gem from Indian literature is sure to mesmerize a new generation of readers.

Read More in Puffin Classics

The Room on the Roof

Ruskin Bond

A classic story of adolescence and coming of age that has mesmerized readers for over fifty years.

Rusty, a sixteen-year-old Anglo-Indian boy, is orphaned, and has to live with his English guardian in the claustrophobic European part of town, in Dehra Dun. Unhappy with the strict ways of his guardian, Rusty runs away from home to live with his Indian friends. Plunging for the first time into the dream-bright world of the bazaar, Hindu festivals and other aspects of Indian life, Rusty is enchanted . . . and is lost forever to the prim proprieties of the European community . . .

Written when the author was himself seventeen, this moving story of love and friendship, presented in an exciting new format with an evocative introduction by best-selling author Anita Nair, will be enjoyed by a whole new generation of readers.